About the Author

S. O. Stephens was born in July 1993. She works for a beautiful company in Tunbridge Wells, and in her free time, she works on her projects. Writing is her passion and when she decided to follow her dreams, she realized that everything is possible when you fight for it. Her dream is to become one of the greatest authors in the world, which she always dreamed of since she was just a child.

The Secret Auction

S.O Stephens

The Secret Auction

Olympia Publishers
London

www.olympiapublishers.com
OLYMPIA PAPERBACK EDITION

A CIP catalogue record for this title is
available from the British Library.

ISBN: 978-1-80074-776-0

This is a work of fiction.
Names, characters, places and incidents originate from the writer's
imagination. Any resemblance to actual persons, living or dead, is
purely coincidental.

First Published in 2023

Olympia Publishers
Tallis House
2 Tallis Street
London
EC4Y 0AB
Printed in Great Britain

Acknowledgements

Thank you to my dearest cousin, Mihaela Sarbu, for helping me with the translation of the manuscript and to my beautiful sister, Flori, for encouraging me.

Chapter One

Like every morning, Emily Growdy woke up to go to the office. It had been a year since she had started working for a company called Old School which sold antiques. Emily worked as a secretary and her job was to stay in contact with all the company's clients. Two days ago, she had been reprimanded by a customer who was displeased by the package he had received. Even though the girl tried to calm him, the mad customer threatened to sue the company, and when all this had gotten to her boss's ears, she was surprised by his reaction.

"Why the hell didn't you give me the phone to talk to him about everything?"

Emily's boss was a tall, strong man with black hair and dark blue eyes around thirty-eight years old. Even though she was working for him, they didn't interact that much. They used to leave messages in each other's offices without paying much attention to each other. But now, she was seeing his anger displayed all over his face.

"But you told me not to interrupt you!"

"I told you not to bother me with any trifles! But you should have known that that problem was important enough to come and tell me! God, if he sues us, we're all going to suffer…"

"I'm so sorry, Sir…"

"Your regrets are useless now! Put me in contact with him now and get out of my sight! I am tired of seeing only an incompetent person in my office all the time!"

Emily left his office completely stunned. She had never been spoken to like that before, and she didn't know what to do. After she finished her agenda for the day, she turned off the computer and went home, but not before leaving an apology note on her boss's desk saying that she would come to the office the next morning, hoping that she would still have a job.

The next day, her boss welcomed her with a smile on his face. He expressed his regrets for how he treated her last afternoon and handed her a check as a sign of gratitude. At first, Emily refused, but her boss finally made her take the bonus. The next few days passed as if nothing had happened…

The morning after, Emily woke up in peace, happy and satisfied with her life. The sun was shining, she was in a good mood, and the thought that soon she was going to have Edward, her little brother, with her, was making her sing and dance with happiness.

When she finally finished her coffee, she hurried to the office, ready for another workday. She hadn't even gotten into the office when she heard her boss's phone ringing and ringing. She tried to ignore it for a while, but finally decided to answer. The girl picked up the phone, knowing that she wasn't really allowed to. In fact, it was one of the rules imposed on her when she got hired: not to enter her boss's office when he was not there and especially not to touch his belongings! The man was obsessed with the order and wanted all the things to be always in the exact place he had left them.

While answering the phone, Emily saw a small black folder left on the desk and began to leaf through it.

"Good morning! I am…"

"Who are you? a thick voice was heard from the other side

of the phone."

"I am Mr. Dalton's secretary, Emily Growdy!"

"And why are you answering his personal phone? Are you that type of assistant that fucks her boss aiming to get a better position?

Emily was full of dander when her gaze fell on the black file, she was flipping through without even realizing it.

"Mr. Dalton must have forgotten his phone on his desk before he left yesterday evening and because it wouldn't stop ringing, I decided to answer. The man's voice interrupted her laughing,

"I wonder how Christian will react when he finds out that his secretary, who is so competent, answered his personal phone."

"Listen, sir, would you like to leave him a message or not?" the girl rushed him, fed up with his intrigue.

"Message you say..." The man's laugh was heard once again, just remind him not to leave his phone at the office again.

Emily was stunned when she saw what was in the file, and after she put the phone down on the desk, she started reading it more carefully. There were dozens of pictures of almost naked women with a lot of information on each girl. The women were numbered, with exotic names, and even though they were well dressed and had makeup on some of them were for sure younger than they seemed to be. Emily couldn't even believe what she had in front of her eyes and didn't understand what her boss was doing with all that information.

Wanting to know more, she quickly took out the small notebook she always had in her tailor's pocket and began to write down some of the names of the girls from the file.

She finished putting the file in its place seconds before she heard the elevator's doors opening and managed to put her notebook back in her pocket just when her boss's angry voice rang out:

"Can you tell me what the hell are you doing in my office?"

Emily winced and stepped towards the door, but Dalton stopped in front of her without moving.

"I…The phone kept ringing… and…"

"You answered my personal phone!" Dalton went to his phone and checked it.

"I thought you were here, and when I saw you were not and the phone didn't stop ringing, I picked it up…"

If looks could kill, Dalton's would have.

"I have never allowed you to enter my office uninvited or answer my phone, much less when I'm not here. You take on responsibilities that do not belong to you, Ms. Growdy. Tell me, what do you think would stop me from firing you?"

Emily flinched at his threat. She couldn't afford to lose her job now that she was so close to taking in Edward to live with her.

"I'm sorry, Mr. Dalton. It won't happen again, I promise!"

Dalton looked at her, satisfied with the power he had on her when he saw the black file. He raised an eyebrow and told the girl:

"When I hired you, Ms. Growdy, I was happily surprised with your shyness and professionalism at work. But I see that things have changed, and now I feel you are more and more curious about what you know is none of your business. It seems that you have forgotten what your job here is and what you were hired for."

"No, sir, please! I promise that it won't happen again and that I won't do anything before asking you first! I am so sorry!"

"I hope so! Otherwise, I would have to take action on this,

Ms. Growdy!"

His ultimatum made a shiver run down her spine. Dalton stepped out of the doorway and Emily walked out of his office to her own.

At mealtime, she saw Dalton heading for the elevator, thinking he was probably going to have lunch, as he did daily. Emily always had her lunch at the office, trying to save as much as possible. She ate the sandwich she had prepared that morning without an appetite, and after that she sat down at her desk and quietly sipped her coffee.

Only when she was sure that Dalton was not coming back did she turn on her computer and open her notebook. She started Googling one of the names from the mysterious file. At first, she couldn't believe what she was reading, but after she searched all the names, she remained silent, thinking about everything she had found out. All those girls were in or around their twenties, from poor families and had been reported as missing, with their parents having no idea about what had happened to them.

Emily kept on reading until she heard the elevator, and in her rush to hide her activities she hit her cup of coffee. The noise of it breaking into pieces made Emily scream in fear, and Dalton, who was coming out of the elevator, came close to her, smiled and sardonically asking:

"Whoever saw you might say you're nervous, Ms. Growdy. Did something happen?"

"No, sir! Everything is all right. I just didn't expect you to come back in such a short time."

Looking at his watch, Dalton said:

"It's four o'clock, Emily. I'm always back at the office at this hour. Didn't you know so?"

Emily blushed and tried to hide the notebook she'd left open on the desk. Dalton kept staring at her, and his question made Emily realize that he was more cunning than she thought.

"Do you work even in your free time?" he asked with his eyes on the girl's notebook.

"I... Emily smiled nervously. I was trying to solve some personal matters. I am sorry to have been using the office computer for my personal benefit without asking you first!"

"Stop being so nervous around me, Emily. I will think that you're hiding something!" Dalton headed for his office and, before closing the door, added:

"If you need anything, do not hesitate to ask me. I'll do my best to help you with anything that is within my power.

"Thank you!" she said, and he closed the door behind him.

Emily fell into her chair relieved. The man was about to catch her searching for information about him. Cautiously, she put the little notebook in her bag to make sure she wouldn't accidentally leave it in plain sight, then carefully gathered all the shards of the coffee cup.

Dalton came out to leave her a list of phone numbers and messages that needed to be communicated to several customers. The man smiled at her then returned to his office, leaving her to work quietly for the rest of the evening. It was the kind of task she had to do almost every day, but now she couldn't help but look suspiciously at the list on her desk. All those numbers that needed to be called and the short messages she had to leave, it was like they were hidden messages. It made her wonder what Dalton was really doing because as far as she could remember, Dalton had never brought any antique object with him or any object that could confirm that the company was dealing with what he said it did. Emily never questioned that, but what she had learned that day made her ask herself hundreds of questions.

The girl also remembered a rather strange conversation she'd had with one of Dalton's clients:

'Hello, I'm calling from Christian Dalton's company. I'm his secretary. Mr. Dalton wants me to let you know about the problem you asked him to solve.'

'I was waiting for Dalton to phone. Tell me, what did you manage to solve?'

'The package is sealed and has been sent off, but Mr. Dalton said that you should be prepared because it is a bit noisy.'

The man on the other end of the phone had laughed. When he finally stopped, he ended the conversation.

'I will be happy to handle this package personally. Have a nice day!'

Emily had hung up and switched to the next person she'd needed to call without asking questions. At that moment, those conversations seemed normal to the girl. When she started working for Dalton, he had informed her of all her duties, and the man warned her that he did not like to be asked questions, or for his secretary to show curiosity about his business. Emily, who was so happy to find a job so soon, had heard enough of his complaints about the last secretary, who asked far too many questions, to persuade her not to make the same mistake. Emily had been grateful to her new boss and had promised him that she would be professional and never to do more than she was assigned to.

And Emily had kept her promise until the day she unwittingly discovered that file on Dalton's desk. She didn't know what to think or what to do next, but she couldn't help but ask herself some questions. What was her boss doing? Who were all those girls? And what did Dalton have to do with their disappearances?

She kept calling the people on Dalton's list and leaving messages, but at the same time, she was trying to find out the truth behind those calls. When she finished the assigned tasks for that day, the girl breathed a sigh of relief and then began to bring order to her messy desk.

She took the papers she had been working with and put them in the paper shredder as Dalton required. After each call, the girl had to destroy all the papers. Dalton had explained to her that they could contain important, confidential information, and the girl didn't ask questions. She just did what she was told to. As she put the paper in the machine, one by one, the girl looked up and winced when she saw Dalton leaning against the door frame of his office, looking at her. The papers fell out of her hand, and Dalton smiled at her.

"I'm done. See you tomorrow morning, Ms. Growdy! Goodbye!"

"Goodbye, Mr. Dalton, have a nice evening!"

"Same to you! And something else, Ms. Growdy… Watch out on the road, it's pretty dark outside and one never really knows who one might meet on the streets at night."

Emily winced because Dalton's words seemed like a threat. Did Dalton know she was questioning his business, and wanted to make her fear for her life? She turned off the computer and left the office, but when she reached the elevator, she went back to Dalton's office and tried the door, which was locked. That seemed strange because she had never seen Dalton lock or unlock the door before.

Emily left for home. She lived a few streets away from her office, and although she could take the bus she chose to walk. She was renting a small house with two bedrooms, a small living room and a kitchen. The house also had a small garden where she liked to spend her free time. She used to plant flowers and take care of a few trees.

When she entered the house, she breathed a sigh of relief. It wasn't until that moment when she realized that she was tense and that at every noise made her look behind her. She took off her shoes, then went to the small window she had left open to ventilate the house. Closing the window, she looked outside, in the dark, she saw something. Fear chilled her to the bone.

On the sidewalk outside her house was someone, who seemed to be a man, staring right at her. She pulled back in fright and quickly checked that all the doors and windows were closed and locked, then approached the window again, but the strange man had vanished.

Emily sat down on the living room sofa, still shaking, and stayed there for a few moments to calm down. She couldn't help herself thinking that the man on the sidewalk had something to do with her boss's advice to take care. But Emily tried to cheer herself up by telling herself that she had seen too many movies and had too many crazy ideas in her head. Maybe the man was walking outside and had stopped to look at something.

Even though she didn't believe much in coincidences, she accepted that that could be one. Maybe the man was waiting for someone right in front of her house, or maybe he was one of her neighbours walking around. After all, she hadn't even seen his face.

Emily calmed down and blamed Dalton's words for scaring her. She took a shower, then made some tea and drank it while watching the news. Her appetite disappeared, and the girl remained on the sofa until she fell asleep. That didn't happen too soon though, because she felt powerless. She was angry because of the fear in her head, and she couldn't find peace too easily.

Her thoughts were flying to Edward, the brother she always wished for, and that one-day destiny had brought her. She took care of him from the first day they met. Emily was ten years old when little Edward, who was only four, was abandoned at the door of the orphanage.

One morning, the little girl, full of energy and joy, despite her condition, accompanied one of the nuns to open the door where someone had been knocking very hard for about fifteen minutes. When they opened the door, a small little human was crying for his mother. Immediately, Emily knew that she would always love that little boy, and from that moment, she took care of him like a big sister and taught him everything she knew. She didn't let the other older children treat him badly, and once, she even jumped in front of one of the nuns, who was slapping Edward because the child could not sleep. Emily then caused a big scandal, after which she was punished and forced to clean the bathrooms for a whole month.

The girl cleaned up without complaining, and she wasn't sorry she did it because she knew she had committed that act to defend little Edward. Before leaving the orphanage, Emily promised Edward that she would wait for him to leave too, and when he did, they would live together. That was going to happen in a few months.

Emily sighed while looking outside, where the sun was starting to shine between the buildings. She wanted to give Edward a better life, security, and happiness, but after the last few days, she was not so sure that she would be able to offer him that. She fell asleep with that thought and when the alarm started ringing a few hours later the girl got up to get ready for work, but she was feeling much too tired. After a hot shower, she had her coffee and dressed up in a navy suit consisting of a knee-length skirt, a three-quarter-sleeved blouse, and a jacket.

At the office, she didn't hadn't even walked in when she heard Dalton talking to another man. Their voices pounded through the closed door, and although Emily tried to hear what the two were saying she couldn't understand it. After a few minutes, the door opened, and Dalton came out with a strange man following after him. He was about forty and massive. The man was bald and had a thick black beard which framed his face. His black eyes and icy look made her feel uncomfortable, and his crooked nose looked like it had been broken a few times. On the right side of his cheek, he had a white scar stretching from his mouth to his ear.

The girl lowered her head as she turned to Dalton, who was looking at her angrily. After the two men said goodbye to each other and the strange man left, Dalton approached Emily and said,

"Looks like you didn't sleep very well last night. You have dark circles under your eyes, and you're trembling!" the man laughed ironically.

"I haven't felt very well lately. I was thinking maybe I could take a few days off…" Emily changed the subject intentionally, and Dalton realized the girl was hesitating to talk about herself.

"I'm afraid you're irreplaceable right now, but what do you say about applying for one of the following weeks?"

Emily approved, and Dalton returned to his office.

For Emily, the days passed as they usually did but the girl seemed more concerned and nervous about her boss's business. Every night when she had to go back home, she had the strange feeling that someone was following her.

The following Tuesday, the girl submitted a request for leave again but received the same answer from Dalton. He could not do without her at the moment. The next morning, Emily did not feel well and asked Dalton for the day off to go to the hospital for some tests.

When she left the office, the girl went to the clinic where she had her appointment while thinking about something else. She entered the building and hid behind a sign. Dozens of people surrounded her. Some were quietly waiting their turn and others were working on computers. She waited a few minutes, and when she wanted to go to one of the counters, she stopped abruptly, trembling.

The man she had seen a few days ago in Dalton's office was entering the clinic's door. The man looked around and as he went to the stairs Emily took advantage of his absence, hurrying to the exit. She got into the first taxi she saw and told the driver to take her to the police station. All the way, she tried to calm down and build up the courage to denounce Dalton.

When she finally arrived in front of the police building the girl was very sure and confident of what she had to do. There was a small office just behind the door and there she saw a young man looking at her with a smile on his face. The man was about thirty, but his green eyes and blond hair gave him a more childish look.

"Hello, Miss! How can I help you?"

Emily looked behind her, scared, then approached the young man's desk and whispered,

"I'd like to talk to someone I can trust!"

The young man smiled encouragingly at her,

"Of course, but first I'll need some details."

Emily looked at him scared and startled when another person entered the building, but soon she realized he was a police officer. He greeted them and then walked to one of the closed doors.

"Listen, someone's following me." The girl looked around

once more, scared, while the young man at the desk was looking at her puzzled.

"What's your name, Miss?"

"My name is Emily Growdy. I'm twenty-three years old, and I live on twenty-one Gosset St."

"Very well, Miss Growdy, can you tell me what you do for a living?"

Emily looked at him in astonishment and impatience.

"Please, I need to talk to someone urgently. He's following me…"

"Who's following you?" The young man raised his eyebrows curiously, and his gesture made the girl feel even more nervous, reminding her of Dalton.

"A man with a scar on his face, I don't know his name… Please, I really need to talk to a superior. Emily paused, and before she started speaking again, she looked around full of fear. I have information about some missing girls. Charlenne Tyson, Danielle Grudwich, Jennifer Bowly, and a few others."

The agent picked up the phone on his desk and dialed a number, after a few seconds he said,

"Sir, I have a person here who claims to have information about Charlenne and Jennifer, the girls who were reported missing a few days ago."

The agent listened patiently for the other person to give him instructions and then dropped the phone and addressed the girl:

"Miss Growdy, follow me, please!"

"Where are we going? The girl followed the young agent down a long corridor."

"You said you wanted to talk to a superior, didn't you?"

The two stopped in front of a door with DETECTIVE GEORGE HALL written across it. The name sounded familiar to the girl. The agent went inside the room and told Emily to wait outside. She sat down on the bench in front of the door, looking at the other doors along the hallway. On each was written a name and in total there were ten offices, five on each side. At the end of the corridor, there was a bathroom next to an emergency exit. Next to Detective Hall's office, there was another door on which was written: CRIMINAL LABORATORY. The walls were light grey with the doors a slightly darker shade. The whole building seemed to have been recently renovated. Emily was kicking impatiently, and no matter how hard she tried to think of other things to ward off her fear, she couldn't. When the officer finally left the detective's office, he motioned to the girl to enter.

"Detective Hall is waiting for you. Come in, Miss!"

Thank you!

Emily entered the room and approached the desk, behind which a man was sitting. The girl held out her hand, and the detective squeezed it lightly, then invited Emily to sit down in front of him. Emily did so and started speaking confidently,

"Hello, sir. My name is Emily Growdy."

"Hello, Miss Growdy, I'm Detective George Hall. Tell me, how can I help you?"

The girl was trembling with fear:

"Someone is following me. I think they found out I know their secrets..."

"Miss Growdy, let's start with the beginning. I'll ask you a few questions, and I want you to answer me honestly. How old are you?"

"I'm twenty-three, Sir."

"Good! Now, please tell me where you live?" Emily carefully watched the man as he wrote down all the details. There was something about him that she didn't like at all. He was a very tall and massive man, with grey hair and blue eyes.

"And where do you work?"

"At Old School Company, Sir."

"What does this company do?"

"I don't know, Detective. When I was hired, I was told that we were dealing with the sale and auction of antiques. Later, I found out some details that made me think, and when I put together all the information, I began to doubt what my boss told me when we first met."

"How long have you been working there?"

"About a year now, sir."

"And for a year, you never questioned your job, Miss? Why are you starting to doubt the company you work for right now?"

"I was warned from day one that I shouldn't ask questions, just follow my boss's orders. Usually, he leaves me messages on my desk that I have to pass on to certain people. I have never seen an antique object there, nor have I personally gone to any auction."

"And what exactly made you start wondering about what's going on in that company now after all these months, Miss Growdy?"

All the detective's questions made Emily's trust in him fade away as the conversation went on.

"I discovered a file on my boss's desk." The girl stopped, and the detective left the pen down on the paper in front of him. He rested his face in his hands and his elbows on the desk.

"And what did you find in that file?"

"The names of some missing girls, and at the same time, I discovered the accounts kept by Dalton, my boss, for the money made by the women who were sold or rented."

"Ms. Growdy, are you aware that your accusations against the company you are working for are very serious?"

"Well, yes... I..."

"And, also, that you could be considered an accomplice if your boss were to be found guilty."

Emily, with a distrustful look, said angrily:

"But I have just told you that I didn't know anything about what my boss is really dealing with. I was just responsible for sending some messages to the customers or for receiving the messages that had to be delivered to my boss. I had no other contact with the customers or with my boss's businesses.

"Ms. Growdy, please go back home and try to calm down!"

"What about the man that is following me?"

"Try not to panic. I will have an agent follow you just to be sure that you are safe, and if someone is following you, we will take him into custody and interrogate him. But you must follow our advice. Go right back home and don't talk to anyone about what you just told us. We will start an investigation against your boss and we'll keep you posted on what we discover about Dalton and Old School."

Emily approved. She felt dizzy, and her head ached terribly. The detective pressed a button and called someone. When the door opened, the young agent entered the room and the detective told him to take Emily to the exit, then handed her a business card,

"Here is my phone number, feel free to call me if you need anything. Go home and leave everything in our hands. We will take care of your safety.

"Thank you, Detective!"

"You're welcome, Ms. Growdy! See you soon!"

The two shook hands once more, and after saying goodbye, Emily was led by the agent to the exit, where she said goodbye to him as well. She thoughtfully made her way to the taxi bay, where she boarded the first unoccupied taxi. After being left in front of her house, the girl carefully looked around, and she did not see any agent or the man who was following her that morning.

She entered the house and went to the small kitchen where she took the biggest knife she had and headed for the living room to carefully look around for anything strange. After rummaging through the house to see if anyone was in it, she felt safer and put the knife back in its place in the drawer.

There was no one on the street then, and to calm herself down Emily prepared a coffee and drank it while thinking about all her problems. It was clear that Dalton was related to the missing girls. And she felt that he was dangerous. The detective didn't seem to believe her, and that didn't help. His questions were quick and harsh and he frequently interrupted her.

Did he know anything about Dalton or the Old School Company? She had to do something as soon as possible. Do something for her own good and Edward's. The boy would soon come out of the orphanage, and Emily promised him long ago that he would live with her. She had promised herself that she would give him security and happiness. How would she explain this whole situation? How could she offer him security and happiness she did not have? What would Edward do if something happened to her? Where would he live? She headed to her bedroom, where she immediately fell into a deep sleep, totally exhausted.

The next day, the girl woke at the same time, and after a hot shower and the strong coffee she always drank. She went to the office where she did her job as always. No one was following her and the girl, though frightened and alert to any noise, was confident that the promised agent was somewhere close by.

Arriving at the office, Emily found the list of numbers where certain messages had to be delivered on her desk. She started the tasks immediately and after she finished, she made photocopies of the list of phone numbers and messages, then put the copies in her bag, careful that her boss would not see her. Then she sent the original copies through the shredder.

Dalton left his office at lunchtime, ready to have his meal. After greeting her politely, he headed for the elevator. Emily waited a few moments and then walked over to his office, entered the room, and approached Dalton's desk, noticing that there was no file.

She opened all the drawers and searched through his papers without finding anything. But she saw a black briefcase next to the desk, and when she opened it she was amazed at the pile of banknotes that the file had covered.

Very nervous, Emily started looking through the file. She was not surprised when she came across some pictures of beautifully dressed girls. On some of them, the word SOLVED was written. When she looked in the briefcase's pocket, she found a passport, and the girl was shocked when she saw Dalton's photo accompanied by the name of another man, Jack Hughes.

She quickly took pictures of everything in the briefcase and then hurried to put it back together. She then left the office and after a few minutes she heard the elevator. Dalton was coming back to work. Emily continued working until the end of the day. Although she was restless and trembling all over, before leaving she passed by Dalton to say goodbye. He invited her into his office, and the girl reluctantly entered.

"Ms. Growdy, I hope that everything went well with your medical tests yesterday!"

"They turned out very well, Mr. Dalton. Thank you for the

question!"

Dalton smiled slightly and stood up, then approached her slightly and whispered:

"Tell me, Emily, what perfume are you wearing?"

Emily looked at him in surprise and replied, trembling:

"I think it's called Vanderbilt, sir."

"I don't think I need to tell you, it smells so good, dear Emily!"

The man was being sarcastic, and Emily felt that he knew she had gone through his things. He was much smarter than he seemed. Dalton came a little closer to her as he stared into her eyes and the girl held her brave gaze until Dalton began to laugh ironically.

"No one can accuse you of cowardice, Miss Growdy!"

Dalton headed to his office where he picked up a sheet of paper which he handed to Emily, telling her

"You told me that you need a vacation!"

Scared, Emily looked at him, unable to believe that Dalton had finally agreed to give her some days off. Something was wrong. Maybe he suspected that she had gone to the police. She took the paper and found that she had the next two weeks off.

"I hope you understand that I can't do without you for more than two weeks, Emily."

Emily smiled forcefully and hurried to answer,

"Two weeks is enough for me, Mr. Dalton." Thank you!

The girl was happy and felt a lot better now that she wouldn't have to be around Dalton when the police caught him. She was confident that in the next two weeks, Detective Hall would find the evidence to prove that Dalton was guilty of everything she suspected.

"I convinced a close friend to take your place for two weeks, but I hope she will do as well as you."

Emily imagined what kind of friend Dalton was talking about while the man continued to talk to her, interrupting her thoughts,

"Do you already have plans for a vacation? Where are you going? Do you have someone close to travel with?"

The girl thought the man was a little too curious about her plans, and Emily congratulated herself for being so reserved about her life. Dalton had no way of knowing about Edward because she had never told him about her personal life.

"I plan to go to the sea for a few days. The salty air will do me good. I don't have many friends or family to notify. I will go alone and take advantage of all the free time I have to rest."

"Oh, I understand!" Dalton raised his eyebrows in a way that annoyed Emily and said slowly:

"I hope you have an unforgettable vacation, Ms. Growdy!"

"Thank you!" said Emily, in a hurry to leave the office. Goodbye, Mr. Dalton!

Emily looked behind once more before entering the elevator. Everything seemed fine. She left nothing there to make Dalton suspect her of investigating him. When she left the building, she breathed a sigh of relief feeling free.

Now it was the detective's turn to do his job. She was sure that after giving him all the evidence she had gathered; the detective would believe her. But before handing the detective all the evidence Emily had to make sure that if something happened to her Edward would have a secure future, at least for a short time until he found his own way in life.

She arrived home convinced that Dalton nor his man was following her, even though she did not see anyone around the house. She was hoping that she would solve this situation before he tried to do something to her. She took out the pictures and information she had and photocopied them. She kept a copy of the information for Detective Hall and put the other in an envelope to keep in case she would need it.

Scared, Emily couldn't manage to sleep that night and instead kept searching the internet for more information about the missing girls and read countless stories about their disappearances as well as about Jack Hughes, who also appeared to be dead. And what terrified her most was that the only Jack Hughes she found appeared to be an old man in his seventies.

She then searched for information about the company she worked for and was not surprised when she didn't find any. When she finally came across a link that contained the words 'Old Factory', the girl found out it was a business from Germany that raised cattle. Emily wrote down all the information she had found out. She didn't know if it would help, but she hoped it would. When she finally fell asleep, it was light outside.

Emily woke up with a slight headache and looked at the clock that showed it was eight-thirty in the morning. The girl had not even slept for four hours, but she managed to stay in bed and, at least, rest a little. When she got out of bed, she smiled at the thought of not having to return to Dalton's office. She prepared a good coffee and, while drinking it, called Detective Hall.

"Hello, Detective Hall on the phone."

"Hello, Detective Hall. This is Emily Growdy."

"Ms. Growdy, how can I help you?"

"I just wanted to let you know that I did exactly as you told me. I continued to go to work exactly as before, and yesterday, Dalton decided to approve the leave I had been insisting on."

"Very well, miss. You better not be there when we start the operation."

"Do you think it will be long before you arrest him?"

"The case is not going too fast. We have no evidence other than your statement. At the moment, we are following a lead, but..."

"I have evidence!"

The detective suddenly was speechless, and Emily continued,

"Yesterday, I was left alone in the company, and I took the opportunity to check Dalton's office, where I found a lot of money, two passports with his photo but different names, and a lot of pictures of the girls that Dalton kidnapped."

"We must meet, Ms. Growdy, as soon as possible! I have a few meetings, but as soon as I'm done, I'll head right to your house."

"I think it would be better tomorrow morning, sir! I must pack my suitcase and buy a train ticket. I'm going on vacation in two days. I feel the need to get away from everything for a time." Emily lied shamelessly.

"You don't understand, miss. You are in danger! Don't go anywhere and don't talk to anyone about the information you have. You could endanger the investigation, and you need to understand that this is a matter of your own security, Ms. Growdy!"

"I have no one to talk to about all this information, sir. I'm an orphan. I don't have family or close friends. It's okay. I'll stay in the house until you come."

After Emily ended the conversation, she hurried to her bedroom, where she quickly changed clothes and then left the house looking for a free taxi, very attentive to the world around her. When the taxi stopped in front of the bank where the girl had a savings account open, Emily hurried to the entrance.

At the counter, she was greeted by a very nice lady who helped her validate her account. When asked why she wanted to withdraw her money Emily lied that she wanted to invest in a friend's business. Although she didn't have any difficulty, when she left the bank, Emily felt insecure and afraid about what she was doing.

She headed for the big park in the middle of London and got lost in the crowd of people. She was attentive to everything that was happening around her, and when she was convinced that she was not being followed, she got lost on the streets until she reached a huge clothing store. She bought a black sweatshirt, a pair of tights, and a hat, which she switched with the dress she was wearing.

After paying for everything, the girl left the store using the back exit and went to the bus station which was a few meters away. It wasn't until she got on a bus, paid the ticket and sat down next to an old man in one of the back seats that she looked outside and saw a man running towards the already-moving bus. It was the same man who had followed her on the way to the hospital. The man she had seen in Dalton's office; the one with the scar on his face.

"Are you okay, Miss?" asked the old man sitting next to her, while staring at her puzzled.

Emily looked at him in turn, scared. The old man probably noticed that she was shaking, and the girl tried to calm down a bit before answering:

"I'm fine, thank you! I hurried to catch this bus."

"Nowadays you find means of transport everywhere, miss. You don't have to run to catch one when another comes right after it."

"I will try to remember that next time!" said Emily while

congratulating herself for her decision; if she hadn't run to catch the bus, she probably wouldn't have realized that man was following her.

Once in the city center, the girl waited for the bus to stop and got off. She continued to walk until she reached the orphanage where she grew up. The house was huge and had about twenty rooms. It was an old building, and some nuns were in charge. Emily knocked on the big wooden door, and when someone answered, the girl felt relief. It was a young, blonde woman with her hair pulled back into a tight bun and wearing a uniform consisting of a blue jacket, matching trousers, a white shirt, and strappy sandals. Emily didn't know who the woman was. She had never seen her before.

"Hello, how can I help you?"

"Hello! I'd like to talk to Mother Davies."

The woman stepped aside, making room for the girl to enter the old orphanage. Emily remembered her childhood in the orphanage in the instant she heard the children playing happily.

"Is Mother Davies waiting for you?"

"No, but I'm sure she'll receive me if you let her know that I'm here."

"If you could tell me your name, I'll go and let her know you are waiting to see her."

"My name is Emily Growdy. I grew up here."

The woman walked away, and Emily took a few steps as she looked around, it was like she could find all her memories there. The front room was the largest, like a large living room. There was the place where Mother Davies used to instruct the children and where the children used to play board games or all sorts of group games. Instead of the small, colorful armchairs, there were huge dark brown leather sofas and a large TV right in the middle of the library full of books. The colorful carpets had been replaced by laminate flooring.

"I remember when you disappeared I always knew I'd find you here. You weren't doing anything special, just sitting quietly imagining things that made you smile."

Emily approached Mother Davies and kissed her on both cheeks.

"I remember that you used to give me a chocolate candy and sit down next to me, telling me stories."

The old woman smiled and took a chocolate candy out of her pocket before handing it to the girl. Emily took it happily, and as she was eating it, she crumpled the paper and tucked it into her sweatshirt pocket.

"Did you come to see Edward? The boy is eager to get out of here."

"I can't wait to see him too, but we need to talk first." The nun looked at her questioningly and, with nod, signaled Emily to follow her. When they reached the nun's office, Emily sat down on the small couch, and the woman next to her grabbed her hands.

"Now tell me, young lady, what's the problem you are facing, and what can we do to help you?"

Emily looked at the old woman, aware of her tenacity in reading her thoughts. The nun was tough but correct at the same time. Emily used to be very close to her and received both her punishments and love, and that's why she had great respect for Mother Davies.

"I need you to promise me that you will take care of Edward, just as you took care of me."

"Tell me what's going on, Emily. Maybe I can help you!"

"You can't! I don't know how I could get out of this!" Emily told Mother Davies everything she had discovered about Dalton, the policeman, and the man who was following her.

"But that detective promised to protect you, didn't he?" asked the old woman, very worried.

"Yes, he promised, but something makes me not trust him too much. I don't know. I have a bad feeling about him. I can't explain why. I just want to be prepared in case things don't go well."

Emily took the stack of banknotes she had out of her bag and handed it to her mother along with the envelope containing the evidence against Dalton.

"I started saving money for Edward to go to college when he gets out of here. I want you to encourage him to do it if I'm not around. And this file... It contains information about Dalton. If something happens to me, I don't want you to go to the police. No one knows about Edward. I haven't told anyone about him, but if anyone finds out things about my life and comes after him, I want you to use that information to protect him. If I disappear, I don't want Edward to start looking for me. I want him to move on with his life!" The girl cried as she talked, and the nun was held her shaking hands.

"Everything will be fine, my little one!" The nun tried to encourage her, but the girl was lost in her thoughts.

"I want Edward to believe that I abandoned him. Yes, you must promise me that you will tell him that, otherwise he'll try to find out what happened to me and I don't want him to get in trouble. Promise me, please!"

The nun wiped the girl's tears and looked her in the eye.

"The police will solve all this, you will see." Emily sighed, and the nun hurried to please her:

"I promise you, Emily, whatever happens, I'll make sure Edward is safe!

The two continued making plans for Edward's future, and when Emily finally calmed down, Mother Davies went to look for the boy. Emily prepared herself, and when Edward entered the room, she didn't look like she had been crying at all.

"Emily!" Edward hugged her tightly in his gentle arms. "I wasn't expecting you until the end of the month!"

"I couldn't wait to see you. I had a day off, and I decided to come forward."

"I'm glad, I have so much to tell you!" Emily looked at him lovingly as he told her his plans for when they would be living together.

At almost eighteen, Edward was taller than Emily. Thin and blond, his dark eyes betrayed his intelligence and sincerity. Emily was proud of him, but she knew that his plans were far from the real life she was facing now.

"No, Edward, you will go to college. You're not going to start working. I'm going to work for both of us!"

"But you don't have to work for both of us. I want to help you. I will postpone college for a while, or I will take some distance learning courses." The boy's face was twisted with pain, but he seemed convinced by his words, and Emily felt sadness. She knew how much he enjoyed learning and how much he wanted to continue his studies.

Emily looked him in the eye and hugged him.

"Promise me you'll go to college! I have the money ready for you to do so, just promise me you will, please!"

Edward looked at her sadly and asked her bitterly:

"How many of your own wishes have you given up to earn this money, sister? How many dresses or shoes did you not buy for yourself so that I could study and not have to worry?"

"It doesn't matter. I did it because I love you. When you got here, I promised to take care of you no matter what. And that's exactly what I had in mind when I started earning money, as you say. Emily smiled, and when the boy smiled back she whispered:

"When you get to be the famous lawyer you want to become, I'm sure you'll buy me a dozen dresses."

Edward lifted her in his arms, then spun her around a few times as they both laughed.

"I promise you sister, I promise I'll make all your wishes come true. One day I will buy you hundreds of dresses. You will be the happiest sister in the world, I promise!"

"Promise me you'll go to college no matter what, my dear, promise me!"

"I will become the most famous lawyer, and you will be the proudest sister." Edward looked at her seriously and said it again:

"I promise!"

The two hugged, and Emily breathed a sigh of relief. By the time she left, it was dark outside. She walked quietly along the road, thinking about all the recent events. When she arrived in front of her house she was still nervous, but at the same time she was calm; knowing that Edward would be safe, in good hands, in case something happened to her.

She entered the house, took off her shoes, then went to the small living room and turned on the light. Her bag slipped out of her hand, and she froze when she saw him. Detective Hall was sitting on the couch in her living room.

Miss Growdy, I've been waiting for you for a few hours, and as you didn't appear, I let myself in.

Emily took a few steps back, trembling. The detective got up and started to walk towards her with small steps.

"We couldn't wait until tomorrow to find out what evidence you have!" The detective waved to the table where all the evidence about Dalton was scattered.

Emily took a few more steps towards the door.

"Tell me, Emily, where have you been until now? Who did you tell about what you discovered?

Emily rushed to the front door and opened it. She shuddered and took a step back, hitting Detective Hall. In front of her was Dalton.

"Hi, Emily!" Dalton came in and closed the door behind him.

"He is... he came after me. You promised to help me!" Emily looked with fear in her eyes at the laughing detective.

"Come on, Emily. Don't try to pretend you're stupid now!" Dalton pushed her face towards the couch. We'd better sit down, George I think we should tell Emily how things really are.

The detective snorted again but stopped under Dalton's stern gaze.

"I knew you were going to get me in trouble, Emily, but I must admit, I didn't expect you to last that long without sticking your nose in my business."

"I think she lasted the longest as your secretary." Hall said as he sat down on a chair.

"None of them lasted more than six months without really rummaging through my office. Only Emily. And I had come to believe that she was the perfect woman until a week ago when I realized she was searching through my files. And yet you resisted for a year, while I patiently waited for you to take the wrong step, while I managed to have control of everything around you without you even realizing it, forming you to my liking. I had even hoped that I'd found the perfect secretary.

"I was betting on you!" Hall approached her while staring at her legs. I always thought you were in love with Jack.

37

The man touched her right leg, and the girl jumped like she had been burnt.

"Tell me, Emily, is that true? Are you in love with me?"

Dalton got up from the couch and approached the trembling girl. He grabbed her in his arms and forced her to open her mouth, then kissed her. Emily was too scared to react, but she bit Dalton's lips in an attempt to make him stop. He screamed in pain and slapped her hard across the face. The girl fell, and tears ran down her cheeks.

"I thought so! She is not in love!" Hall grinned as he grabbed her hair and dragged her to the couch. "I won the bet, Jack, so I'll take my prize. The detective picked Emily up and slammed her onto the couch, and then sat down next to her. The girl's lower lip was bleeding, and she had a red mark on her right cheek.

"Ever since I saw you, I wanted to do this!" The detective squeezed her breasts lightly, and the girl moaned in pain.

Dalton approached them and pulled Hall away from the horrified girl.

"We can't do this, George! The girl is untouched, and you know very well that this will bring us double the reward."

Hall swore, and after pushing Dalton away from Emily, he said angrily:

"Let me play with her another way. I don't have to be her first for her to satisfy me. You know that!"

The man walked over to Emily, who hit him in the head with a vase she took from the coffee table. Hall fell by the couch, and the girl ran to the front door and tried to open it, but the door was locked, and the girl began to look for the keys in the bag she had left on the small shelf from the entrance. Dalton approached her and rattled the keys in his hand.

"Is this what you're looking for, Emily?"

"Please let me go! I promise I won't tell anyone about you. I will disappear. Let me go, please. I promise you will never hear from me again!"

The girl shuddered at the noise of the keys hitting the floor and hurried to pick them up while Dalton sat against the wall, relaxed. When she turned to the door to unlock it, Emily heard footsteps behind her. When she turned back around, Dalton was right behind her with his hand on her neck. Emily dropped the keys and turned to Dalton to hit him, but he caught her with one hand, while with the other put a handkerchief over her mouth. Emily smelled something sweet and felt faint, staggered, and without realizing it, she fell into Dalton's arms.

Chapter Two

Emily felt like her head was going to explode from the pain in her scalp. She tried to open her eyes, but the dizziness that gripped her made her close them again. Her nostrils were stinging because of the strong smell of dirt and rot. She heard footsteps approaching but remained silent.

"Did she wake up?" Emily winced. The question was asked by a man with a thick voice.

"She didn't show any signs. Are you sure you didn't use too much chloroform?" The question was asked by a female voice. The two people reached her, and a fine hand began to measure her pulse.

Emily smelled Dalton and recognized his voice. Recent memories came back to her, and all the events before her fainting replayed in her mind.

"I don't think so. I used the dose I always use, not an extra gram."

"Then we wait for her to wake up, and when she does, we start training her. When did you say the next auction would take place?"

"About a month from now..."

The voices receded, and it was hard to tell what the two were talking about. Emily opened her eyes and looked around. The room was lit by a lamp on a small, rusty table. Next to the lamp was a glass of water and two slices of toast with margarine. Emily tried to get up because she was thirsty, but her legs felt powerless and she let herself fall back on the dusty mattress. Within a few moments, she was asleep again.

"Wake up!" Emily felt like her hand was shaking violently and opened her eyes.

"Who are you?" Emily asked slowly while she remembered that the woman who now was sitting quietly in front of her, had already come to her with Dalton before.

The woman was blonde, with long wavy hair in a ponytail. She wore dark blue eyeshadow and black mascara that made her eyelashes appear to reach her eyebrows. Her lips were bloody red. She didn't look tall, about one meter sixty-five, and her body was well proportioned. Her breasts were perfect, not exaggerated by her size, and she seemed to have implants. They were highlighted by a red dress, tight and short which made the woman's legs look longer than they were. She was wearing high-heeled shoes, and their golden color matched her jewelry.

"My name is Julia, and I think you already understand why you're here, right?" The woman looked at her impatiently, and her attitude made Emily afraid.

"I remember I was home with Detective Hall." Emily was shaking, and her face turned white as she spoke. Then Dalton appeared and told me I could leave. He gave me the keys, but he came after me at the door, and before I could leave, he put something over my nose and I fainted. I'm in the hospital, right?

Julia laughed and contemptuously told the girl,

"Do you think I look like a nurse?" She turned around and headed for the closet where there was a lamp, and started playing with the switch. "Do you think this room looks like a hospital ward? You're wrong, my dear. You could hardly believe that this was a hospital."

41

"I heard you talking to a man. It was Dalton, wasn't it? Dalton is the one who kidnapped me."

"So, you weren't asleep?" Julia approached the girl's bed and pulled on the sheet that covered her. Emily was standing naked in front of her.

"Where are my clothes? What did you do to me? Emily was trying to pull the sheet out of Julia's hand."

"I haven't done anything to you yet!" Julia turned to the door, which she opened, and a tall, thin man handed her a red satin robe and a matching pair of slippers. Julia turned to Emily and handed her the clothes.

"Get dressed. You will soon find out what you are here for. We will start preparing you for what is coming immediately."

Emily, who squatted in the middle of the bed, startled.

"Get me ready for what? I want my clothes back!" The girl jumped at Julia and tried to knock her down but did not manage to. The door opened and a man pulled her away, holding her hands. Julia stepped forward and slapped her hard as she shouted,

"Stupid! Never do that again. I assure you you'll regret it! Andrew, help me with this bitch. I was sure she wouldn't cooperate!"

"Please don't hurt me, Julia, please!" The girl's sighs grew fainter as Julia injected her with a syringe in her right hand, helped by Andrew.

Emily lay softly in the man's arms, and he supported her while Julia dressed her in the red robe. Then they headed for the elevator through the dimly lit hallway. When they reached the elevator, Emily saw Julia pressing one of the buttons and then the elevator moved.

The three stepped into another hallway, which was much brighter and very nicely decorated. It was much bigger and cleaner than the one they had come from. There were two huge black armchairs on the right and a small table placed in front of them. On the walls behind the armchairs there were some rather shameless paintings showing the bodies of naked women, chained to those of men, in various positions that did not seem comfortable or satisfactory.

Julia headed for one of the doors along the hall, a door marked MEDICAL OFFICE. When they entered, the first thing Emily noticed was the man sitting behind the massive wooden desk. He was about fifty years old, his gray hair gave him a pleasant air, and his brown eyes looked at her gently. The man smiled at her, then motioned for the girl to sit on the white bed.

"Hi, Emily. My name is William!" The man approached her and frowned as he studied the red spot on her cheek. He turned to Julia, who was sitting quietly by the door, and snapped at her:

"Why did you hit her?"

Julia started laughing softly as she looked at the two of them.

"I don't have to give you any explanation, my dear. Jack gave me free reign in her training."

"Still, I don't think he'll be so happy to see marks on the girl's face."

"They will fade before the auction, William. Stop exaggerating!"

"They'd better disappear. Otherwise, you know what consequences we will have to face with Dalton. Wait outside now!"

Julia's smile disappeared, and the woman left the room, followed by Andrew. Emily was left alone with William, who put on his gloves while talking to her.

"You must stay calm. Don't move or tense up while I do my job here!" William approached her and, with one hand, began to move the girl's legs away, while with the he other held her still. He inserted two fingers into her vagina, carefully moving until he reached a certain point where he stopped, then withdrew them gently. When he finished, he took off his gloves and threw them in a sterilized trash can.

Emily rose to her feet and then headed for the chair in front of the desk. William smiled contentedly at her and motioned for her to sit down. Emily did so, ignoring the fact that the robe didn't cover a quarter of her body or the man's eager gaze.

"Do you think they will kill me?" Emily asked, scared.

"kill you!" William appeared amazed by the girl's question. "Who would want to kill you and why?"

"Dalton knows; I found out everything. I know about the missing girls and the fact that he is selling them. And Julia beat me." Emily was crying. "I heard someone talking about an auction, and that I had to be prepared. I knew they were going to kill me. I discovered all his secrets…"

"You're valuable, my dear, and I'm sure Dalton won't touch a hair on your head now that he'll find out he wasn't wrong about your virginity."

"My virginity? But what does this have to do with Dalton?" Emily looked at William in disbelief.

"They didn't tell you why you were here, did they? The man continued to talk when the girl shook her head. They will put you up for auction and sell you to the one who will be willing to pay the most for you."

"But why will they want to pay a lot of money for me?"

-"They drugged you, didn't they?" The doctor looked sadly at the innocent girl. Listen to me, girl, and I really hope you'll remember when you get out of this state of euphoria. You have two chances! The first and the hardest would be to get out of here.

Many have tried, and almost none have succeeded. And the second is to accept what will follow and not resist Julia's or Dalton's demands, or you will end up dead. These two will not hesitate to hurt you at the slightest denial on your part. Be careful…"

Julia entered, not bothering to knock on the door, and interrupted William.

"What happened, William? You decided to taste her first?"

"Don't talk nonsense, Julia! You'd better let the girl rest! And she'd better drink something. She's dehydrated."

"Before that, I want you to know what you found out."

"The girl is untouched, but we have to wait for the test results to find out if she has an infection or anything."

"I don't think she has something like that. From what Dalton said, the girl was tested regularly. If she had an infection, she would have treated it."

"And yet it would be better to make sure. The people we work with would not be very happy if they got an infection from the girl they bought from a brothel."

Julia started laughing and pulled Emily's hand and then pushed her towards the door.

"Since when do you care about buyers, William? I thought Dalton and I were the ones taking care of them. You never agreed with what was going on here, did you?" Julia went out without waiting for the man's answer, and after closing the door, saying to Andrew, who had already caught the girl in his arms,

"Take her to her room and force her to drink water. I left a few bottles in her room. Remain outside her door unless you have something more urgent to do!"

"Okay! Should I also start giving her ecstasy?" Andrew waited for the answer.

"No, wait and see what Dalton says."

Andrew entered the elevator with the girl. Emily looked at the man's the scarred face, and his crooked nose made her think he had been a boxer or had dealings with beaters. His small brown eyes were shining, and his big mouth smiled at her.

"What's your name?" the man asked.

"Emily. Yours?"

"Andrew."

The two looked at each other without letting any feelings appear on their faces.

"Thank you for taking me in your arms earlier. I really couldn't stand up."

"I was just following Julia's orders. I know she seems like a bad person, but she is not. At least if you listen to her, she will treat you well. You have to accept your fate and do what they want. You won't get out of here."

"This is not my fate! It is the one you want to impose on me while forcing me to give up my real life." Emily rushed at the man and began punching him in the chest. The man let her release all her anger, and when he felt her soften and heard her cry, he hugged and comforted her.

"You must be strong and do what they want if you want to survive, and maybe one day you will be able to get out of this business."

"I don't want to survive. I want to die." The girl's shoulders sagged with pain. The elevator stopped, and the two stepped outside. Before entering the girl's room, Andrew said,

"Do it for your family, if not for yourself. Survive for them!"

Emily remembered little Edward. She couldn't believe she had forgotten about him, probably because of the drugs. Or maybe it was better to forget about him. For him, she no longer existed. She had told Mother Davies to tell the boy that she had died in an accident if one day they could not contact her.

"I don't have anyone, I don't have a family. I grew up in an orphanage."

"So, did I." The giant's smile was sad. It wasn't very pleasant!

Andrew opened the room's door and, with a nod of his head, told her to enter.

"I must shut you up again. I am so…"

"Don't say that. You're not sorry. If you were really sorry, you would help me out of here!"

"I can't do that, little one. This business is more than it seems. You, me, William, even Julia, we're all puppets in the hands of powerful people." Before closing the door, Andrew whispered to the girl, "You will get out of here. I do not know which the best way is to do it. All I know is that it will be much better than if you had stayed with Dalton.

Emily was left alone with tears streaming down her cheeks. She missed Edward, Mother Davies, the orphanage, and all she hoped was for Dalton to never make the connection between her and Edward. She couldn't fight him, and now that she could put together what she'd learned from Julia and what she'd discovered in Dalton's office she knew she was going to be sold at auction, and no one would look for her again. Tired and sick of crying, the girl rested her head on the pillow and fell into a deep sleep.

"Emily, wake up!" Andrew was holding a tray of food in his hands. On one of his shoulders was an article of clothing made of lace and black velvet. Emily looked at him, puzzled. She got up while Andrew was putting the tray next to her on the bed.

"Julia sent me to tell you that after you eat, you have to get ready. She sent you this dress to wear."

47

"I'm not hungry." Emily felt how dry her mouth was, and although she was hungry, she felt nauseous at the same time.

"You have to eat. If you get sick, they will kill you!"

"I don't care, I don't care! I don't want to eat. You can get the tray out of here." Emily pushed the tray down, and it fell, rolling the fruit and food on it to the floor.

Andrew dropped to his knees and began to wipe off the soup that had left a yellow stain on the light-colored parquet with a napkin.

"Get dressed. Dalton is upstairs and wants to see you. He is in a good mood, and I advise you not to change that!" The man spoke harshly.

"For my part, Dalton and Julia, and everyone can go to hell!" Emily pulled on the lace of her dress. Andrew tried to take it from her hands, it was too late. The material was torn.

"Emily, don't do this, please!"

"Andrew, wait for us outside!" Dalton was carelessly leaning against the doorframe, staring at the two of them. No one heard or saw him when he arrived. Andrew looked at the girl once more before leaving, and Emily crouched on top of the bed.

Dalton closed the door and began to take off his belt.

"What do you want to do? Let me go, Dalton, please! I promise I won't go to the police anymore."

"I think you deserve a little punishment, Miss. Show me your hands!" said Dalton watching her with anger.

"Please, Dalton, don't do it!"

"You should have thought about that before throwing the food on the floor and tearing the dress Julia sent you. Show me your hands!"

Emily was crying while trying to get away, which only made Dalton angrier. The man pulled her hair, brought her to the edge of the bed, and then began to hit her with the belt. The girl screamed in pain. The strap touched the corner of her mouth, and Emily tasted blood. Dalton's face twisted with hatred. Emily had never seen so much evil in anyone's eyes.

"Will you show me your hands now?"

Emily held out her hands and tried to swallow her sobs.

"This is because you threw the food on the floor." Dalton hit her with the belt over her right hand, then, when hitting her over the other hand, he yelled at her,

"And this is for the dress."

The man continued to strike her a few more times, then tightened his belt and put his belt back on. Emily's hands were swollen and stinging, and a thin stream of blood ran down her fingers. Dalton laughed at the girl's pain.

"Tonight, you stay in your room and eat what you can find." Dalton motioned to the tray where the food Andrew had gathered from the floor was, then continued:

"And tomorrow you will start training with Julia. You'd better listen to her. Otherwise, I'll be back, and I promise I won't be as gentle as I was today!" He said before leaving.

Emily heard the door opening, and then Andrew approached her, looking at her with pity.

"I'm sorry. I didn't know Dalton was there."

"If you were really sorry, you would help me get out of here." Emily cried and screamed at the man who was trying to calm her down.

Andrew took her hands and began to wipe them with a small towel, which he'd brought from the bathroom. After cleaning them, he began to apply an ointment to her wounds.

"I have a family. A wife and two children. If I help you or if I break any of the rules, they will kill my family."

Emily looked him in the eye, and she thought of Edward and Mother Davies. She probably would have done the same thing if she had been in Andrew's place. She would have protected her family at all costs.

"How did you come to work for them?"

When I started working for Dalton, he told me he had a brothel and needed me to look after the girls. I agreed, but after a while, I realized that Dalton's business wasn't exactly legal. He kidnapped women, whom he later sold or forced into prostitution. When I wanted to leave, I wasn't allowed. They said I knew too much, and that once you get into the business it's not so easy to get out. They keep threatening me. Do you understand? They know everything about my family and believe me they will not hesitate to kill them if I take a wrong step."

Andrew pulled the tray closer to the girl's bed. He put the cream on the nightstand next to it, then left the room. Emily tried to get out of bed but couldn't. She dropped back on the bed and, tired of crying, closed her eyes in pain and weakness and fell asleep again.

When she woke up, her hands were stinging terribly, and her head rumbled. She was hungry, and she reached for the fruit tray. She took an apple and chewed heavily. The corner of her mouth hurt because of the wound. After finishing the apple, she managed to swallow a few mouthfuls of water from the glass next to the tray.

Andrew entered the room and took the tray, then put another in its place, which contained a cup of coffee, two croissants, margarine, and jam.

"I am sorry!" Emily said hoarsely. Andrew, who was preparing to close the door, turned his head and smiled at her.

"You'd better get ready! Julia will come to see you soon. If you need anything, knock on the door."

Emily nodded, then began to sip lightly from the bitter coffee as she thought of a way out. She got up and put her red robe on. The girl heard the key twisting in the door and then Andrew appeared and looked at her, amazed.

"I'm ready!" Emily seemed more confident. "Take me to Julia!"

Andrew led her to the elevator, and when the doors closed behind them, he asked her briefly,

"What are you going to do?"

"I'll find a way out of here alone."

"It's impossible to get out of here. The last time someone tried it didn't end very well. They will kill you!"

"At least I'll end up dead and not sold to who knows who! said Emily trembling with anger."

"Listen to me, Emily!" Andrew grabbed her hands and forced her to look him in the eye, then continued. There are girls who were sold, and after they got out of here, they had and still have good lives. They are rich and having fun in exotic countries.

"But I don't want money, Andrew. I don't want to sell my body for money. I don't want to be at the mercy of a man who will mistreat me. You don't understand! This is not life…"

The doors opened, and when the two saw Julia approaching them, they dropped the conversation.

"I was just coming to get you. I see you got ready earlier!" Julia smiled at the girl.

"I'm ready for the lessons you told me about yesterday."

Julia raised her eyebrows, amazed.

"Very well, follow me!" Julia moved towards one of the rooms in that hall and when she stopped in front of one, Andrew hurried to open it. Julia turned to him and said,

"You're free for the rest of the day. You can take advantage of the time and go see your family."

Andrew said goodbye after thanking Julia and then left.

Julia came in and motioned for the girl to follow. The big room was beautiful, a large bed was in the middle of it. Next to the huge closet was a golden makeup table. On it, there were many deodorants, perfumes, makeup, and jewelry.

"This will be your new room from now on. Julia walked to the bathroom door and, after opening it, told Emily,

"Here is the bathroom. Go in and take a shower. I'll wait for you!"

Emily didn't make Julia say it twice. She felt the need to remove all the mess of the last few days. The water whipped her, and the wounds on her hands and face stung on contact with soap. The girl rubbed the sponge until she felt her skin becoming raw. When she came out, she found a towel hanging on the shower door. She wrapped herself in it and looked at her face in the mirror.

The mark Julia had left was almost gone, but her lip was still swollen and she had a small cut in the corner of her mouth. Deep circles framed the girl's eyes, and her gaze seemed blank.

"Emily, get out of there, or I'll have to call someone to break down the door!"

Emily unlocked the door, and Julia entered the bathroom in a flash.

"Never do this again. You don't have to lock the door. No one would come for you. Put this on!" Julia handed the girl a white robe, and Emily put it on, then came out of the bathroom. Julia was waiting for her in front of the makeup table.

"Sit down!" Emily did as she was told without comment, and Julia began to apply a cream on her face.

"Why are you doing this?" Julia stopped for a few seconds then continued.

"We like our girls to look good so that when we auction them, the profit will be as high as possible."

"I wasn't talking about the makeup."

Julia answered after a few minutes of staring blankly,

"At first, I was just like you. Innocent and young. They brought me here when I was sixteen years old. I had no family to look for me. I had no one to miss. They treated me well, sold me to a man, but he quickly got bored of me and after a while, he gave me back. When I got here, I asked to talk to the boss, and when he finally accepted, I made him a proposal that he could not refuse."

"What was it?"

Julia smiled contentedly at the makeup she had applied.

"I did a good job, didn't I?"

Emily looked in the mirror, amazed. The shrill makeup made her look completely different. She didn't like herself at all. It changed her too much. Her eyes were bright pink, she had a thin, black line on her eyelid that ended in a slight curve and made her green eyes look mysterious, her eyebrows were too sharp, she thought, and her lips were too red. Her cheeks were highlighted with pink blush, and Julia had given the girl a fine outline to her face. Emily raised her hand to her face to wipe her makeup, but Julia stopped her.

"In a few days, your face will no longer be covered in bruises, and you will be perfect. In the meantime, I'll teach you some makeup tricks. Put on this dress, and let's go.

Emily put on a yellow dress that fell in waves over her thin, tall body. The deep cleavage fit the girl's small breasts nicely. Julia added a gold chain around her neck with a small butterfly pendant. When they left the room, Emily saw several girls walking down the hall. They were all nicely dressed and fashionably arranged. None of them looked around. None of them said anything.

They walked through that hall for a few meters then turned left, and after a few more meters Julia opened a door and the two entered. It was a beautiful room. The walls were covered in beautiful photos of women. A few colored sofas in shades of pink and white surrounded the room, and in the middle, there was a table full of magazines and books.

The small office caught the girl's attention and she headed to it. There was only one photo on it depicting a laughing child.

"Is this your child?" Emily turned to Julia, who was looking for something in one of the office's lockers.

"Yes!" Julia took the photo of the girl from her hands and put it back on the desk. She pulled Emily to one of the armchairs, and when they were both sitting down she opened the file she was holding, pulling out a photo. "She is Catherine. With our help, she got her hands on an Italian billionaire. Now she is on vacation spending her husband's fortune." Emily looked at the photos with distrust. They were of a very beautiful blonde woman sitting next to an old man. The woman was well-dressed and poised, and although she seemed to be surrounded by luxury, the look in her eyes did not express happiness.

"And this's Amber. The girl managed to find her better half with our help." A gorgeous brunette was sitting next to a man in his forties. The man held her tightly around her waist, and although the girl was smiling too, it did not reach her eyes.

"And yet none of them seem really happy, even with all the wealth around them, their smiles are fake."

"Maybe at first, they felt that way, but after a while, they got used to it. They realized that with these men, they have security and wealth, something they would never have had if they had stayed in the environment in which they were born." Julia spoke harshly to the girl.

"If you say so… But tell me, what happens if I do not accept this situation?" Emily gestured to her clothes, to her face, to all the pictures.

"You'd better accept it. These girls are among those who did well. I doubt you want to know what happens to those who refuse to listen to us. Follow me!" Julia was relentless, and the girl continued to follow her until they reached a double door. Julia came in, the door creaking behind her.

"This is the dance and music room." Emily looked at the room, which was made up of mirrored walls. Several instruments were placed in one corner of the room, and the one that caught the girl's attention the most was the piano.

"Why are we here?" Emily began to walk around the large room.

"This is where you will spend an hour or two every day, depending on how much you want. You will be lucky enough to learn how to dance or play an instrument."

"All this for what? How will it help me?"

"Men do not only want women to look good, they also want women who know how to speak in society or how to dance. They are more attracted to a woman if she has talent and education."

"Who are these men you're talking about?"

"Powerful, rich people. Men who are used to having what they want." Julia slowly stroked the piano keys and the sound they made resounded in the empty room.

"Tell me, would you like to try an instrument?"

"In the place where I grew up, there was a piano."

"You grew up in an orphanage, didn't you?" Julia raised her eyebrows questioningly, then continued, "How come you didn't make any friends?"

Emily's heart was pounding. She didn't want to talk about the wonderful people at the orphanage. Instead, she sat down in front of the piano and began to play. When she finished, Julia started clapping.

"That was beautiful. You are so good at this!"

"Moonlight Sonata by Beethoven. The director of the orphanage taught me to sing. She was a good woman who treated me well. She died before I was eighteen, and that made me want to leave. I could have stayed and helped, but I didn't have anyone to support me there, so I decided to leave." Emily got up from the piano and smiled at Julia, who looked at her with pity. The girl knew that Julia was faking kindness and hoped she would never find out the truth.

"Everything will be fine, I promise! From now on, no one will treat you badly. We will find you a good man who will treat you like a princess."

Emily wanted to kill the bitch in front of her, but instead, she smiled at her. She had to play their game if she wanted to get out of there.

"Let's go. It's dinner time. I hope you like fish. Our chef is preparing it right now. Julia went into the hall and walked around talking about what they were going to eat. Emily took the opportunity to study all the rooms they passed. At the end of the hall, Julia opened the door to the staircase. The girls went down a few steps until they reached a floor with two doors.

"Here's the kitchen." Julia entered the room, with Emily following her closely. The kitchen was equipped with everything that could be needed, like industrial cooking appliances. The girl couldn't help but wonder why they needed a cook and all the sophisticated appliances. When they went out through the swinging door the girl understood why. At the huge table were about twenty chairs.

"I asked for food to be brought to us now. You're probably hungry. We both know that you didn't eat much the other day. We usually have breakfast at ten o'clock, lunch at two o'clock and dinner at eight. Tomorrow you will meet the other girls." Emily listened as she studied the room.

A TV was on one wall while a blackboard was on another. Next to it was a small table on which were boxes of chocolates and other assorted sweets. The girl's gaze ran to the only painting in the room. A naked woman lying on a black sheet and a man sitting on top of her with his head between her legs. The woman had a spasmodic face and a slightly open mouth while her hands were caught in the man's hair. The man's hands were on the woman's breasts.

"Do you like it?" Julia asked while filling two glasses with wine.

"It's an interesting room." Emily came closer to the table where a man was just putting down two plates of fish and vegetables.

"Thank you, Pedro!"

The man nodded and left without saying a word.

Emily stood by the door, and as she looked out of the small window behind her, she smiled contentedly. Next to one of the refrigerators there was a black door, probably one of the exits. Julia told the girl to sit down at the table and handed her a glass of wine.

"I don't drink, thank you!"

"Men appreciate when the woman he goes out with drinks a

glass of wine with him." Julia put the glass down on the plate in front of the girl, then sat down at the table and began to sip slowly from the fragrant wine.

"What if a woman doesn't want to drink?" Emily was not able to understand all the things Julia wanted her to learn and the rules she wanted her to follow.

"It is a sweet wine with the aroma of graft, guava, wood, and blackcurrants. It's called Sandbar if I'm not mistaken." Julia took the bottle in her hand and looked at the label. Yes, it's really called that. Then she continued. "Cosecha 2014 Lymbay[1], is one of my favorite wines."

Emily looked at her astonished and asked herself if it was really necessary to learn all those details. They were going to sell her. And even if those lunatics were behaving like some prepared and understanding teachers, the girl knew that it was a brothel, not a school for girls. The girl was puzzled, but her thoughts were interrupted by Dalton's arrival.

He came through the kitchen, and the raindrops in his hair confirmed to Emily the idea that there was a nearby entrance, maybe even the black kitchen door she had already noticed.

"Hello!" Dalton took off his black coat, dropped it carelessly on one of the chairs, and then turned to the girls, looking right at Emily. "But what do we have here? Stand up, Ms. Growdy, let me clear my eyes with your beauty." The man was slightly sarcastic, and Emily remained still without moving in her chair, looking down. Dalton approached her, grabbed her hand, and then pulled her toward him, forcing her to stand up.

"You look better than I was expecting. Men will go crazy when they see your beautiful body." Dalton began to caress her

---

[1] Harvest 2014 Lymbay

lips slightly, and Emily winced as he touched the small cut with one of his fingers. Dalton laughed and kept talking. "I didn't want to be so harsh with you, but I had to punish you."

Emily raised her head and looked at Dalton with hatred.

"You're a wretched man! I hope you rot in hell!"

Dalton burst out laughing again and went to Julia, who he kissed for a long time. When he finally pulled away, he sat down next to her and looked at Emily.

"I'm sure that the one who will take you will be happy to have you."

Emily headed for the kitchen door, but before she left, Julia stopped her and brutally pushed her towards the table.

"Sit down and eat! And you'd better get used to Dalton. He comes and goes whenever he wants. He's the boss here."

Julia seemed angry, so Emily sat down while trying not to look at Dalton laughing hoarsely. Being so nervous, Emily took the glass of wine and drank it in one gulp. The cook came with a plate of food, which he put in front of Dalton. The three ate quietly, and when they finished, Julia stood up and asked the two if they wanted coffee or tea. Dalton said yes, and Emily shook her head, wanting nothing more than to leave the room.

"Emily plays the piano." Julia began to tell Dalton about the girl's talent.

"If she does everything so well, she won't do badly in her new life." Dalton stared at the girl's cleavage, and Emily trembled as she looked at him with hatred.

"How did the tests come out?"

"Everything turned out perfectly. Emily is a virgin, exactly what you always believed. She hasn't been touched by any man."

"A diamond in the rough!" Dalton raised his eyebrows. "Maybe I should keep her for myself. Who knows, maybe I will get to be her first."

"If you touch me, I'll kill you!" Emily got up angrily, and Dalton started laughing.

"Go to your room! Tomorrow we will start your classes." Julia, in turn, stood up and looked at Emily with hatred in her eyes. Emily was able to see the insecurity behind the hatred.

Julia pressed a button on the keyboard embedded in the wall, and within minutes, Andrew appeared.

"Andrew, would you please take Emily to her room? Be careful not to leave the door of her room unlocked."

Emily followed the man, and when they reached the hallway, she asked him:

"How is your family? Did you manage to see them?" Emily was looking at the man with envy, but she was still trembling because of Dalton.

"Yes, I managed to see them. My children grow up too fast, and my wife never stops blaming me for not spending enough time with them."

The two continued to walk silently. Before opening the door, Andrew asked the girl:

"Are you okay? You seem different. Did Julia manage to convince you that what she is doing is for your own good?"

"What is being prepared for me is the only way out of here. Or, at least, that's what Julia says." Emily looked defeated, and Andrew grabbed her hand. Before pushing her into the room, he said:

"Read it inside and be careful to destroy it." There are surveillance cameras everywhere. Emily felt when Andrew put something in her palm and then shook her hand lightly.

She went to the bathroom and turned on the water in the shower, then opened the crumpled paper.

I'll help you. Emily's heart raced. She tore the note, then flushed it down the toilet. She got in the shower and cleaned all the cream off her body. Then she washed her face, removing all traces of makeup.

She fell asleep that night with hope in her soul and her thoughts of Edward and what they would do if she managed to escape.

The next day, Emily woke up optimistic. She had a shower, and while humming one of her favourite songs. She tried to put her thoughts in order. She had to follow Julia's advice and make her think she was okay with all her ideas. Andrew would help her escape, and the girl couldn't wait to hear his plans. She continued to hum in the shower, aware of the cameras she had discovered last night. One in a corner next to the closet and the other hidden among the perfume bottles. Emily put on as much makeup as she could and put a tight, knee-length black dress on. She didn't have much to choose from in the closet full of bold dresses.

When Julia entered her room, she was amazed.

"Looks like life here is starting to suit you!"

"Anything that could help me get out of here as soon as possible!" Emily said.

"Should I understand that you are ready for today's lessons?"

Emily agreed and held Julia's gaze, who seemed satisfied with what the girl was saying.

"Follow me! We had breakfast an hour ago. You don't receive anything until lunchtime. Here we do not tolerate whims. If you skip mealtime, it is your problem, you must know that you will not receive another meal instead."

The two of them went to the elevator together, and a few moments later, when it stopped, Julia walked forward and opened one of the doors, and the girls waiting outside entered. The room was dimly lit, and twenty one-person desks, all with chairs, were arranged in four rows. In front, there was a desk and on it a laptop and a projector. On the front wall was a blackboard with a cabinet next to it. Julia turned on the light, and Emily saw a black box next to each table. Black velvet curtains hung from the windows, preventing light from entering.

"Sit down at the first desk on the right!"

Emily headed over to where Julia told her to sit down and stared at the door, which opened from time to time. The girls who entered the room did not look older than she was. One of them seemed familiar to her, and Emily studied her closely.

Her hair was short and freshly dyed a dark shade of red. She had too much black makeup around her gorgeous blue eyes, and her big, full lips were bright pink. Emily remembered her. Her name was Charlenne. She was one of the missing girls. The girl looked much thinner than in the photos found in Dalton's office. She wore a black leather mini skirt and a white sleeveless top that didn't cover much of her large breasts. Emily continued to look at the other girls, but when Julia began to speak, she had to look back at her.

"Hi, girls. Today we have a new colleague. Her name is Emily." The girls looked at her, some with interest, others as if she were an intruder. Emily managed to hold their gaze for a while until Julia took the black box and put it on the table where Emily was sitting, then started talking to them:

"Please take out the big object first. Most of you know what it's called or how to use it. But as we have new people among us, we will repeat the exercise once again."

Emily was amazed as she stared at the object in front of her, unaware that there even existed such a thing. Of course, she knew what it looked like. When she was still living at the orphanage, she used to help the nuns when they bathed the younger children. When searching on the internet for something, there were occasional spam messages with images of a man's genitals. The books she had read sometimes contained details of what can happen between a man and a woman when they liked each other.

The object in front of her looked different. It wasn't real. It seemed like it was made of some kind of plastic or silicone, and it was soft and thick. The head resembled a mushroom, with a small cut in the middle and thin, strange skin.

"It's called a penis." Emily looked up at Julia, who was watching her intently. "If you press the red button next to the right testicle, you will notice how the penis starts to change from a soft shape to a hard and stiff one."

Emily pressed the button and saw that what Julia had just said was starting to happen. The vibrator became stiff and longer.

"Put your hands on it. Feel it!" Julia took Emily's hand and forced the girl to put it on the shaking vibrator. "This is what really happens when you touch a real penis. From the shape of a splashing mushroom, it becomes a hard stick."

Some girls burst out laughing, and Julia continued to talk:

"When a man's penis gets hard, it means that he is horny, and we all know that the only thing he wants at that moment is to have sex."

Julia approached the table, and after pressing some buttons on the laptop a few times the projector turned on. Images of a blonde woman appeared on the front wall. The woman was wearing a white satin nightgown that showed off her pink nipples and tiny panties of the same color. The woman was walking slowly towards a man sitting on a chair.

He was dressed in a black robe, and after the woman untied the sash around his waist, the man was left naked. The blonde woman reached for the man's genitals, which immediately hardened. She caressed him lightly with her hands. The man got up and started kissing the woman as he removed all her clothes.

When the two were undressed, the man took the woman in his arms and propped her against the wall. He put his penis in between the woman's legs. They moved faster and faster, moaning, and when they finally finished, the woman let her head fall on the man's shoulder.

Julia paused the movie and turned on the light. Emily was shocked by what she had seen and, at the same time, curious that a woman and a man could become so intimate and close.

"As you can see, the union between a man and a woman is very pleasant. Many of you already know how it feels. It's something exciting that will make you want more and more. I hope you enjoyed today's lesson. Before long, you will be just like the woman in the images. You will tremble with pleasure in the arms of a man we will choose for you. You can retire now. Go to your rooms or the gym if you want."

Julia smiled mockingly at them, and the girls began to leave. Emily took advantage and went out with the other girls. She leaned against the wall while waiting for the elevator and breathed a sigh of relief when she saw that Julia was not following her.

"It's not so pleasant! Especially when you come across a beast like the ones we are forced to be with. You tremble in pain, and they don't care about how you feel." The brunette laughed and looked at Emily with some sort of anger.

"Shut up, Tiffany!" A blonde, petite woman in a short denim jumpsuit said. The girl had long hair and an angelic face.

"Why should I shut up? This girl needs to know that nothing is how they want us to believe. It is not about our pleasure here.

For us, it's only suffering and pain."

Tiffany was a brunette and quite tall. Her hair fell in waves down her back, and her black eyes were sly. She had a pale pink eyeshadow on that matched her lipstick. She was dressed in a tight, knee-length pink dress.

Next to them, there was a Caribbean girl with curly hair and coffee-colored eyes. She was wearing a lot of makeup and a long white dress that left her back bare. The girl had a bruised face, and Emily could read the pain in her eyes.

"Nobody is here for pleasure, Tiffany. Leave Emily alone and don't scare her anymore!" Charlenne came closer, looking with reproach at Tiffany as she continued saying, "We are all obliged to do what they want."

Suddenly, the girls stopped talking as they heard a door open.

"What's going on out here, meeting between whores?" Julia asked. "Are you planning something that I should worry about?"

"I was trying to get to know Emily better and give her a pleasant welcome!" The brunette shook as she looked at Emily pleadingly.

Julia raised her eyebrows, and Emily agreed.

"Very well, then if you're done, go to your rooms and have a rest. See you at dinner! Emily, wait five minutes. I have to talk to Charlenne, and then I'll take you to your room.

The elevator doors opened, and Andrew stepped towards them. "Andrew, you're here! Please take Emily to her room. The girl doesn't know the building very well." Julia left with Charlenne, and Emily got into the elevator with Andrew while the other girls went in other directions. When the elevator doors closed, Emily burst into tears and grabbed Andrew's shirt.

"Please help me get out of here once and for all. I have

money. Help me, and I promise I will give you all I have. Please!"

Andrew pushed her away, and the girl hit the wall behind her.

"If you don't keep your distance, I'll tell Miss Julia what you're asking me to do!"

"But you told me…"

"Stop it! Andrew grabbed her by her arm and shook her hard. I don't want to hear you!"

Emily remained silent, being scared of Andrew. When they reached her room, the man unlocked the door and pushed the girl into the room, not before shoving another note into her palm. Emily headed for the bathroom, where she began to cry as she read the note. You have to be patient! I'm working on a plan!

Emily flushed this note as well. She washed her hands and tried to wipe away the mascara that was all over her cheeks. She came out of the bathroom and went to bed, where some books had been placed. The girl read their titles: Sex Every Day: 365 Positions and Activities, 11 Minutes, Flat Sex.

Emily took the books and threw them aside as her thoughts flew to what had just happened in the elevator. She had to be more careful with what she talked about and when. There were cameras in the elevator and probably everywhere in the building.

Andrew had reacted too violently, and the girl was aware that he had lost his temper out of fear. He must have known where the cameras were placed. She had to wait for his messages without approaching him. Otherwise, she would only bring problems to Andrew, which was the last thing she wanted to do.

Time was passing quickly, and when she heard a knock on the door, she was startled. She had to go to dinner, and if she were late, Julia would not have been happy. Andrew opened the door, and Emily walked past him with a smile. The two made their way to the kitchen without speaking.

The girls were all seated at the table, along with Julia and Dalton. Emily entered the room, and Dalton got up and held the chair for her to sit down. The girl winced as he put his hand on her shoulder and she tried to pull back, but Dalton squeezed her tighter and whispered in her ear:

"One day, you'll thank me for everything I do for you, and you will no longer look at me with hatred. You look great today!"

Dalton retired, and Emily sat down in her chair, looking at the napkin in front of her. The food was brought out as Dalton served wine to the girls.

"It's a dry wine, Crianza[2], made from a grape variety called Cabernet[3]." Tiffany said the words confidently and proudly at the same time.

"True, the wine is called Laudum Crianza[4], the year is 2009. Very good, Tiffany!" Julia clapped her hands, pleased, and the girls started to do the same.

Emily forced herself to eat the turkey breast with baked oranges while Julia told Dalton all the girls' achievements.

Dalton was looking at each of them while trying to bring them into his conversation with Julia by asking them questions. It seemed to Emily that Dalton was trying to get the girls to trust him. He was behaving as a friend would, not as a man forcing

---

[2] Crianza is the first tier of a "Reserve" wine. Spanish law requires that for a red wine to be labeled as a Crianza, it must be aged for two years, with a minimum of one year in an oak barrel and for another year in the bottle before it's sold.

[3] Cabernet Sauvignon is one of the world's most widely recognized red wine grape varieties.

[4] A Red wine from Alicante, Valencia, Spain. Made from Cabernet Sauvignon, Merlot and Monastrell.

them to sell themselves.

Emily didn't know how the other girls ended up there, but from Charlenne's words, she had understood that they were all forced into prostitution. Emily saw Charlenne smiling back at Dalton at that moment and couldn't help wondering how the girls could accept him. Was she lying or just pretending to accept the life she was forced to live? As soon as the coffee was brought, Emily got up and asked permission to retire to her room.

"Sit back in your chair. No one leaves until we all finish our coffee!" Dalton gave her the order as he looked at her provocatively.

Emily sat down and forced back her tears. She turned to the girl on her right and tried to strike up a conversation.

"What's your name?" She asked in a whisper.

"Chelsea," answered the girl after a few moments. Emily noticed that her hands were shaking when she took the cup of coffee to her mouth.

"Who did that to you?" Chelsea almost dropped the cup, but set it lightly on the table, and instinctively put her hand to her bruised eye. "It was him, wasn't it?" Emily looked at Dalton.

"Please stop! If he hears us talking, it'll be worse for me."

Emily did as the girl asked, but the conversation between the two made Dalton curious, he asked Chelsea,

"Did something happen, Chelsea?"

"No!" the girl answered dryly, with a trembling voice.

"I wanted to know if she could lend me a pen and a few sheets of paper. I have to take notes from the books I have in my room." Emily told Dalton, gnashing her teeth.

"You can ask Julia anything you want, Emily!" Dalton smiled at the girl and then turned to Chelsea. "And you, Chelsea, go to your room and get ready. We're going out tonight." Chelsea agreed, and as she stood up, Emily saw the girl's pallor and the fear in her eyes.

Dalton got up too, followed by Julia, who ordered Andrew, who was just entering the room, to take the girls to the locker rooms and gave him a training plan.

The locker room was huge. On one side, there were lockers. The other side was covered with mirrors, and the middle divided by wooden benches. The girls opened the closets where there were tights, socks, panties, sports bras, sweatshirts, and many other kinds of sports clothing. Everyone was choosing which model they wanted, and it didn't seem to bother them much that Andrew was right there next to them. Some seemed to even enjoy being watched. As they changed clothes, they looked at him with smiles on their faces.

Andrew, instead, was looking at Emily. When the last girl came out of the locker room, and they were left alone, he approached her and whispered:

"In a few days, I'll have everything ready, and I will get you out of here. Now change your clothes and go with the other girls. Julia will be here soon. Don't give them reasons to hurt you. Be strong!" Emily wanted to hold him in her arms, to feel that what the man was saying was true. She needed to hear that everything was going to be fine. She was exhausted and feeling more and more like she would soon collapse.

Andrew went out, and the girl picked up a random sweatshirt, a pair of tights, and sneakers. When she entered the gym, the girls were looking at her in a strange manner. Some even laughed as they saw her too-big sweatshirt and tights.

Andrew, handing out worksheets to the girls, handed her one too and began to explain how the fitness equipment should be used. Emily started using a device called an elliptical machine, and after a while, her legs started to hurt because of the way the sneakers squeezed her feet. But she continued to do what Julia, who had arrived there in the meantime, was telling her to.

After about an hour, Julia told all the girls that they were free to retire to their rooms after taking a shower. As on previous occasions, she asked Andrew to take Emily to her room, then she left.

When she entered the locker room, Emily noticed the door to the showers. She entered and took off her sneakers, seeing all the wounds on her legs. Charlenne came in behind her, naked, followed by a few other girls, and when she stopped at the mirror in front of her, Emily noticed the scars on her back too. They were long and black and looked like whip lashes. Tiffany caught her observing her marks while she was looking at Emily's back too.

"It is said that Dalton enjoys hurting disobedient women. Charlenne was a little naughty when she was brought here, and Dalton had to tame her."

"You're a fool!" Emily said, defending Charlenne, who hurried into one of the showers, crying.

"You're a prude!" Tiffany shouted.

Andrew entered the room, and the girls fell silent. Emily walked away from them and decided to take a shower in her room.

After taking a shower, Emily noticed the marks on her feet. Next time she had to choose a pair of sneakers more suitable for her. As she applied her body lotion, she thought about what Tiffany had told her about Dalton having big plans for her. She had to get out of there as soon as possible!

Chapter Three

Emily sat down at the table and looked around. The place next to her was empty.

"Where's Chelsea?" Julia, who was still calm, looked at the girl and while she was analyzing her, she raised her coffee cup to her mouth and sipped from it, then she answered:

"Chelsea doesn't live here anymore!" she said while putting the cup back on the table. You should eat. We will start the lessons soon.

Emily tried to eat, but her thoughts did not give her peace. Where was Chelsea? What did Dalton do to her last night when she told him to get ready to go out with him?

The girls' conversation was only about the outfits and makeup they were wearing. Emily wasn't talking to anyone. She was afraid to do it again. Chelsea hadn't wanted to talk, but she'd insisted. Now Chelsea wasn't there anymore and no one was saying anything about it.

Julia stood up, and the girls followed her to the movie theater where they were going to learn new ways to please men. Before entering the room, Emily saw Andrew. They didn't know it, but Julia was watching them.

When the girls were all sitting down, Julia urged them to take the vibrator out of the box and then headed for the projector. She turned it on then inserted a DVD into the laptop.

"Today, we will learn that we can give pleasure to our

partner. Julia pressed a button on her laptop, and the movie started playing."

A young brunette entered a bedroom where a naked man was laying on a bed. The girl was wearing a leather underwear suit, panties, and a bra. The woman came closer and began to touch the man's sex. When it hardened, the woman replaced her hand with her mouth. She was licking the man's penis, and she was moaning when she took it in her mouth. The man was pulling her hair and pushing harder and harder into her mouth, moaning and vibrating with pleasure. The man screamed when he finally finished and let the liquid dripping from his penis run down the face and mouth of the smiling girl.

Julia stopped the video and started talking to the girls:

"Blowjobs are a very practical method that is used to give pleasure to your partner. Of course, the situation can be reversed, and the woman can be the one who receives pleasure, or they can both offer pleasure at the same time. Oral sex is quite common nowadays and is very satisfying."

Julia pressed a button on the laptop once more. In the next video, the man had his head between the woman's legs, and her hands were stuck in his hair as she pushed her hips forward. At one point, the man sat on his side with his head still between the woman's legs and his feet on her head. The woman began to kiss the man's penis while he licked the small bud between her legs. Julia began to speak:

"Press the vibrator button!" Julia approached Emily, who was sitting at her table, quietly, looking at the other girls. She turned on the sex toy. The position you see here is called position sixty-nine and allows the mouth of each partner to play with the sex of the other. Now you can practice fellatio with the vibrator in front of you.

Julia returned to her table and took out a vibrator as well. After turning it on, she began to caress and lick it.

"Imagine that you are next to a man, and you want to give him pleasure." Julia swallowed almost the entire plastic penis and occasionally let out a moan. The girls began to do the same.

Julia looked up and observed the girls. She saw Emily looking at the floor, and she got mad. Julia got up, approached her, and slapped her hard across the face.

"You'll do what I say if you don't want Dalton to know about your attitude. I'm pretty sure he'd be more than happy for you to practice with his dick. Now put this into your mouth!

Emily did so, and Julia reached into the girl's hair, pressing her down hard. Emily couldn't swallow it, and couldn't breathe, but Julia continued to push her head down. When she stopped doing it, the girls started laughing at Emily, who was coughing and crying.

"The lesson is over. Go to the locker room and change! See you in the gym!"

Emily hurried out of that room and headed for her own, fed up with Julia.

She threw herself onto the bed and continued to cry. Julia seemed to find pleasure in humiliating her in front of other girls just because she liked to see her reaction. She was enjoying the hatred and the anger she could provoke in others. Emily wanted nothing more than to die because she didn't think that she would ever escape from there. When Andrew entered the room, he found her crying and full of despair.

"You have to go to the gym classes. Julia sent me for you!"

Emily began to tremble nervously; her face was white and her eyes screaming for help.

"Help me get out of here, please!" The girl started screaming hysterically as she clung to Andrew's neck.

The man has pushed her away from him and slapped her. His reaction made her look at him full of reproach as she managed to stop crying.

"Go to the bathroom, wash your face, change your clothes, and let's go!

Andrew went to the closet and took out some of the clothes he had given her. Emily went to the bathroom, and did exactly as he ordered, and right before leaving the bathroom, she noticed a little piece of paper on the floor.

You'll be out of here soon. Do as they say until then! Emily flushed the note. She didn't know what to think of Andrew anymore. Now he was slapping her and treating her badly and then he was promising her he would help her escape.

As she studied herself and all the marks on her body in the mirror, she decided to do exactly as the man wrote in the last note. She had to be smarter than Julia if she wanted to get out of there, and she wanted that at any cost. She wiped away all the tears still running down her cheeks and smiled at her image reflected in the mirror.

Andrew knocked on the door, and the girl walked past him, smiling with gratitude. They headed for the gym, and when they got there, the girls were already properly dressed and sitting at some fitness equipment. Julia smiled at Andrew after looking at Emily, who had a red face.

"So, the girl needed a boost to get to where she was supposed to be!" Julia said, and a hateful gaze appeared on Emily's face, who turned her head. "Go to the next free bike. I'll be right there!" Emily walked to where Julia indicated, and Julia told Andrew. "If it wasn't so important to Dalton, I would have been more than happy to teach her a lesson."

Julia laughed at what she said, and Andrew did the same as they were both looking at the girl's tense back. She had just heard what Julia said.

"Why is this girl so special?" Andrew asked.

-Don't you know? Julia asked, with her eyebrows forming an arch over her eyes black as coal. Dalton has some new clients, and they are willing to pay a real fortune for a girl who has never been touched. They are good guys, part of high society, guys who always want to have the best, and it seems they can't wait to play with a virgin. Emily is one, and on top of that, she also has this captivating beauty she was unaware of until now. Many would kill to have this beauty with long, brown and curly hair, big green eyes and brown skin and Dalton says that this will bring us a lot of money. Julia looked at Emily enviously. The girl was really very beautiful with her harmonious body and angelic face and a smiled that was making her shine every time. The girl was about six foot tall and thin; she didn't need the gym, in fact almost none of the girls there needed to go to the gym, but that was Julia's way of keeping them busy.

"How is your family, Andrew?" Asked Julia bored.

"Okay, the kids go to school and Diana takes care of them and of the house. They're all fine!" Andrew looked confused, he felt Julia's question was completely out of place.

She was never asked personal questions and the fact that she did now, when he was trying to get his family out of the country, made him think that something was wrong.

"I'm glad, I hope it will all stay that way!" Julia walked away and Andrew was left alone with his thoughts. He felt Julia's words were a threat and could not congratulate himself on the plan he had decided to follow that very morning. His family was at that time on a plane with his brother, they were heading to

Romania, the country where his beloved wife was from. The man had planned this together with his brother and he knew that soon he was going to follow them, but first had to save Emily. The girl was too innocent, her eyes expressed too much pain, and he knew that if the girl continued there, she would not resist what those bastards were preparing for her.

After the girls quietly had dinner, Julia asked for coffee. Emily felt tired, and she was slowly massaging her aching hands. The other girls were talking, and Emily envied them because she didn't understand how they could behave as if nothing was wrong there. They all seemed satisfied and agreed with the life they were living.

Dalton entered the room at that moment.

"Good evening!"

Julia stood up and kissed him lightly on the lips.

"Good evening, Darling!" Julia said while taking his coat and hanging it on the rack. "How was your evening?"

"Everything went exactly as I expected!" Dalton smiled and pulled Julia towards him. "At the end of this auction," the man said while his gaze was going from Emily to Julia, "We'll take a little vacation, and we'll go to Florida for a week, what do you say?" Dalton started kissing her, and Julia touched him all over as she responded to the kiss that seemed to never end.

"I think it's perfect. Everything is perfect! The woman was in the heaven staring at Dalton."

Emily didn't know the two were together, but seeing them now, she thought they were made for each other. They both had something that scared her. Dalton walked away from Julia and poured himself a glass of wine, then turned to Emily.

"The police closed your case. It is rumored that you disappeared with one of your lovers. You left the rent unpaid and only a few clothes behind."

Emily gasped, and the color disappeared from her cheeks. She wondered who'd reported her as missing.

"It was not so hard to make you disappear without a trace, apart from the owner of the house you were living in, who kept insisting that you were a serious girl. No one appeared to notice your absence. I didn't think you didn't even have a friend or someone close to you. And the owner of the house was quite easy to manipulate. She ended up telling herself that she should have thought twice before renting the house to an orphan."

Dalton burst out laughing and made a toast with Julia. The other girls were silent, and none of them dared to look at the two people in front of them. Dalton took an ID and a new passport out of his coat pocket and threw them on the table in front of Emily.

"Emily Growdy died the moment you were declared missing. These documents are yours!"

Emily looked at the documents. The girl in the picture was her, but she did not recognize herself. Her hair was cut short and blonde, and the make-up made her look much older.

"One day, you will pay for everything you're doing now!" Emily looked at him with hatred.

"From now on, your name will be Chloe Turner. I think it suits you!"

The two looked at each other with hostility, and Dalton was the one who, bored, turned to Julia and continued talking to her.

"Dinner is over. Send the girls to their rooms. We both have something to celebrate!"

Julia did just as he said, and although she was happy to celebrate with Dalton, the woman was jealous as she watched Dalton and Chloe facing each other. Ever since the girl was brought there, Julia had felt Dalton's interest in her, and she knew that although the girl was already promised to someone, Dalton could always change his mind and make her his woman. This thought terrified Julia, she would never lose Dalton to another woman, she was the only one who accepted and understood his needs. And if Dalton ever decided to leave her for another woman, she would destroy him and the one he chooses. Chloe was making Dalton lose his mind. Not many girls had the guts to challenge him because they all knew what he was capable of doing when mad. The man's sadism was revealed whenever he felt provoked and although Julia accepted the state of affairs, lately she felt the man's violence becoming more and more fierce. Dalton was the king of sadists, he was happy to cause pain to the women he was with, sometimes he hit them so hard that it took them a few days to recover. Julia was upset because she knew the man was attracted to Chloe, she had noticed his reaction when she was answering in disgust. That was exciting Dalton, and Julia, although she knew she was the one who always satisfied his perversions, knew that he was thinking about Chloe. Julia told the girls to leave and followed Dalton to his bedroom.

When she wanted to open the door, Dalton grabbed her in his arms and kissed her lightly on the right ear as he rubbed against her. They entered the room and Dalton walked with her in his arms, until he reached the table full of makeup and perfume bottles. He removed them with one hand and slammed Julia hard on the heavy wooden table. She gasped in pain and Dalton began to kiss her brutally, biting her, making her lips bleed. When she wanted to get away, Dalton slapped her hard on the face and started laughing as he twisted her hair. Julia gave in knowing that Dalton wouldn't hit her if she didn't resist, her dress was ripped off while the man was strangling her with one hand, making her cry in pain.

"I like to fuck you so hard, you're the only one who knows how to satisfy my needs." Dalton whispered her words as he thrust his cock deep into the woman's vagina, while she wasn't able to breathe because of the hand that was suffocating her. Tears were falling down her face from pain and frustration. She tried to bite his hand, but Dalton took his hand from her mouth and began squeezing her breasts hard, biting and scratching them with his beard as he dug deeper and deeper into her body. Julia felt dizzy as Dalton, who had lost control, slapped her hard on the face once more. He moaned loudly and let himself fall over her with Julia being frozen in pain. Her blood was dripping lightly from the corner of her mouth, and she was full of anger. She pushed Dalton away, got up, and headed for the bed.

"Did something happen?" Dalton asked as he pulled his trousers on, seeing Julia whose face was twisted with pain.

"If you ever touch me like this again, I'll kill you!" Julia looked him in the eye and Dalton began to laugh.

"You have never denied me pleasures, what's happening now? You know you cannot expect romance from me!"

"You've never been so violent with me before and you know that. I don't want what happened to Chelsea to happen to me too one day."

Dalton came closer and gently wiped the blood from her mouth with one finger, then looked her in the eye and whispered:

"You don't have to worry about what happened to Chelsea that night. I could never hurt you so much. I love you!"

Julia winced softened, it was the first time Dalton had told her he loved her. She had fallen in love with him a long time ago and that is why she always accepted his perversions. Tonight, she had almost fainted from the pain he caused, but his statement delighted her beyond measure. The man began to caress her breasts gently and the woman's gaze changed, she moaned slightly, and Dalton kissed her as he removed her clothes. Julia unzipped his pants and then pulled them until he got rid of them. Then, he continued with the shirt that landed next to his pants, then the man climbed next to Julia in bed and began to kiss her neck, as he came down to her breasts touching her between her legs. He made love to her, refraining from abusing her in any way and the woman fell asleep a few minutes after she had an orgasm. Dalton watched her as he was getting dressed, making no noise. He thought it was a shame that Julia was beginning to aspire to his love because he wasn't capable of love, he was the type that got what he wanted, when he wanted it, no matter who was going to suffer. The woman's jealousy annoyed him; he didn't like women putting limits on him. After getting dressed, he walked out of the room, smiling. He would get rid of Julia; the woman knew too much and was not like the other girls. She was smart and able to cause trouble. She had to be eliminated, maybe even sooner than he wanted to. Dalton was planning to satisfy his most hidden desires with her while in Florida, then he'd kill her.

"Chloe, wake up!"

The girl sat up and looked around, it was dark, and she was trying to figure out who was talking to her. She turned on the light near her bed and met Julia's gaze. The woman's eyes were swollen from crying. She had dry blood on the corner of her mouth, and her face was pale. There were bruises on her cheeks and mascara all over her face.

"Julia, what happened? Who did this to you?"

"It's your fault! Dalton loves me." Julia jumped into the girl's bed and began to shake her, pull her hair, and hit her cruelly while shouting at her. Chloe started screaming and struggling to escape the woman's claws because it seemed that Julia had gone crazy.

"Julia, stop, please!" Julia didn't seem to hear anything and just kept hitting her.

Andrew entered the room and hurried to pull Julia out of the bed.

"Julia, try to calm down!"

Julia was crying now and staring blankly. Chloe looked at her with pity. Even though she had hurt her, she couldn't ignore what the woman's situation was like because of Dalton.

"He does not deserve you! Look at the state he put you in." Julia looked at her, and Chloe managed to read the distrust in her eyes, and she kept talking:

"You deserve more than a bastard who beats you. Look at you!"

Julia pulled herself out of Andrew's hands and headed for the door.

"I tripped over a chair. Dalton would never hurt me. He loves me." The woman hurried out of the room, and Andrew grabbed Chloe in his arms. The girl was trembling, her face was white, and she looked extremely scared.

"I'll do everything I can to get you out of here as soon as possible. I promise you, little one!" Andrew whispered into her ear.

Chloe sighed and hugged him tightly until she stopped shaking. Andrew laid her on her back in bed, wrapped her in her fluffy blanket, then turned off the light and left the room.

Chloe didn't manage to sleep that night, and not in the nights that followed. Every time she came close, she woke in tears and at the memory of Julia's hateful look filling her mind.

The days went by just like before. The girls woke up in the

morning, had breakfast, were forced to go to the gym to perfect their bodies, and were forced to watch porn to learn the art of sex. Julia hadn't shown up since that evening and Andrew went everywhere with the girls.

Chloe was struggling to fall asleep when she heard a light knock on the door, and then she heard it open. The girl shuddered and clenched her legs. She was afraid and prayed for it not to be Julia or Dalton. She could no longer stand them.

"Chloe, wake up! It's me, Andrew!"

The girl breathed a sigh of relief. She got her head out of the blanket and looked at him sadly.

"We have to hurry. It's time to go! I've turned off the cameras."

Chloe jumped out of bed and hurried to get dressed in the clothes Andrew had brought: a pair of black tights, a black T-shirt, sneakers with a cork sole, and a hat to hide her face.

"How did you do it?"

"I found the right moment, if I can say so, but we have to hurry. We don't have much time. I managed to turn off the cameras for an hour. The alarms are turned off and so we will have no problem using the garage to get out."

The two left the girl's room together and went down the stairs to the basement.

"What are we going to do?"

"Once we get out of here, we'll head to Den Helder . I think it's the easiest way out of the country without exposing ourselves to the world too much."

"But I can't leave the country, not without…"

"You have to! Dalton has more power than you can imagine. He'll find you wherever you'll hide."

"But I have someone here!" Chloe stopped abruptly. "I can't

leave him alone again. If Dalton finds out about him, he'll kill him."

"Listen." Andrew grabbed her hand and shook her slightly. "Dalton knows all about you. He has been investigating. If there is really someone in your life, you will keep him safe if you disappear for a while."

Chloe looked him in the eye and saw the fear on his face. She agreed and followed him to the garage. Reaching the basement, they turned left into a small hallway. The two were not speaking, they were instead attentive to any noise around them. They went out into the garage using the emergency door that led to the underground parking lot where there were several cars. A black Mercedes, Class C, a BMW 5 series, a red Mini Cooper, and a white Ferrari. Andrew headed to the Mercedes, and the girl almost ran as she tried to keep up with the man who was nervously talking:

"I can swear I saw Dalton leaving, and he never leaves without his car."

They reached the car and got into it. The girl breathed a sigh of relief as she sat in the comfortable seat and fastened her seat belt while Andrew whispered incessantly to her:

"We have little time left, and we will be free!" He took the girl's hand in his and smiled encouragingly at her.

He turned the key, but the car wouldn't start. The man started swearing and looked at the dashboard of the car, which showed that the tank was empty. It was not possible. He had filled it that morning. He got out of the car and headed for the next one. The BMW was locked, so he returned to his car and took out a hammer. He started hitting the locked car's window, and after a few blows, it broke. He reached through the broken window and opened the door, then removed the shards.

He motioned for the crying girl to get into the BMW, then tried to make contact with the wires he had removed from under the steering wheel. Eventually, the car started, but the steering wheel was locked. The BMW alarm had not sounded, as it should, the Mercedes tank was empty, although he had filled it up that morning. Something was wrong.

"It seems that the cars are not useful at this moment, we will walk to the exit. Take care and follow me. Something doesn't smell right to me."

The girl followed him, and when they were almost at the garage door, they heard footsteps behind them. They moved faster, but their path was cut off by one of Dalton's men, a beast. Andrew pulled out the gun he had on his belt and pointed it at him. But there was someone behind them clapping, and Dalton's laughter echoed in the garage:

"You've come a long way, haven't you?"

Chloe turned abruptly, scared. Dalton's gaze made her body tremble. They were cornered. They, Dalton and his two men, had guns. The girl felt like fainting. She was paralyzed with fear.

"Andrew, Andrew! What should I do with you? You knew what would happen if you betrayed me, and yet you chose to do it." Dalton laughed loudly, then continued. "And you were so stupid to think I wouldn't realize you would. You thought you could hide your family from me. You disappoint me, my brother, you should have at least learned something from me after all the time you were with me."

Andrew pointed his gun at Dalton.

"You can't reach them. I sent them away from you!"

Dalton came closer and showed him a picture of his wife and children, the photo was taken in a yard, and the three looked happy as they played. They were probably in their new home, and Andrew suddenly looked afraid and angry.

"Are you sure? This picture was taken two days ago. It seems that your wife settled quite quickly in your new house in Romania."

"Don't hurt them, please! The man's shoulders dropped, and his voice was begging for mercy. You have me. I did you wrong, not them!"

Andrew was immobilized by the two men, who rushed at him and grabbed his arms as he fell to his knees. The man struggled, but he was already defeated and worrying about his family. Chloe looked at him in pain and fell on the cold cement, overwhelmed by Dalton's hatred. She looked at him as he pointed the gun at Andrew's head and continued to throw painful words at him.

You once swore to me that you would be loyal to me as long as I needed you and I promised you that your family would never lack anything. I promised to take care of them. Why did you have to betray me for a bitch?"

"She is not like the others. She is innocent…"

"There are no innocent women. You know that very well, brother!"

Chloe suddenly raised her head and looked at them. It was the second time Dalton called Andrew 'brother'. She could now see the resemblance between the two, but she didn't want to think that they were siblings. Dalton was far too bad, and Andrew had just risked his life to help her.

"Don't hurt them, please. I am the one who betrayed you. They are your family. Andrew looked at the picture with adoration and pain as he was crying. He is your son, for God's sake!"

"I never gave a damn about my family, and as for my alleged

son, you might be right."

Andrew struggled to escape the hands of the two beasts, but with no chance of success.

"Fuck you, you have always denied everything! Diana denied it too when I asked her, but I heard her talk so often while sleeping. And when she started begging me to stop working for you, I knew something had happened between the two of you. Why did you do it?"

"Your intuition never deceived you, Brother. Diana was my woman, and she enjoyed it. I can assure you of that."

"You raped her. You were always jealous of everything I had. You always wanted to be above me. You raped her because you knew she was my wife."

"I assure you that she enjoyed it. I can still hear her screams and moans of pleasure." The man laughed hoarsely as he watched Andrew cry. "As for the family, our mother was a notorious and abusive drunk. She always enjoyed hitting me, and while she cared for you tenderly because you were younger, she beat me excessively and sent me to get money for her drinks."

"It's not my fault. I never agreed with her. You know I always asked her not to hit you. I couldn't do more!

"You're right, it wasn't your fault. It was her fault, and that's when I bought my first gun. I came home and emptied it into our mother's body. Now it's time to take care of you too."

"No!" The girl's horrified scream was overshadowed by the sound of Dalton pulling the trigger.

Andrew fell to the ground, and Chloe ran towards him, took his head in her arms, and put him on her knees.

"Take care of them, please!" Andrew finished his last words with difficulty and closed his eyes as he took his last breath.

"Call an ambulance. Emily was cried and screamed

hysterically as she looked at her bloody hands. "You're a murderer. Why did you do it? I hate you! He was your brother! Why?"

Dalton fired a few more shots into Andrew's lifeless body, making Emily scream in terror and run away.

"You, go after her and take her back to her room! And you, take care of this corpse!"

Dalton gave orders to the two men, who didn't even blink as Andrew was cruelly shot, put the gun back in his back pocket, then walked quietly to the stairs leading to his office. He was smiling and seemed pleased with himself.

Chloe reached her room and dropped into her bed. Her legs trembled, and Dalton's men terrified her with their presence. As she was trying to close her eyes, she saw Andrew's lifeless body and the blood all around him. His last words resounded in her ears. The girl screamed in pain and helplessness. Her mouth was dry, and her throat stung, but she didn't care. She wanted to forget everything that had happened; all the pain that consumed her and didn't give her peace.

Someone was shaking her and telling her to shut up. Julia was looking at her with pity, and the girl fell silent.

"Stop screaming like you're crazy! Julia told her harshly. It's your fault. If you hadn't lured Andrew to your side, Dalton wouldn't have killed him."

Chloe started screaming again, but Julia slapped her face, and the pain made her stop immediately. Julia was happy that she had decided to follow Andrew. She had noticed the signs he and the girl were making to each other when they thought no one was looking at them. She took care to put a microphone in the phone from the man's car and so she found out that he was trying to get his family out of the country. In the last few days, she carefully watched the video cameras that had been installed throughout the building and had even installed one in the girl's bathroom. She knew about the notes she was receiving from Andrew, and also that they would try to escape that night. That's why she decided to tell Dalton everything and he managed to empty the tank of the car that Andrew usually drove and set a trap for him and the girl. Julia was so proud of her having managed to save one of Dalton's belongings. The man would show his gratitude and the holiday that he had planned for them was going to be the beginning of a more open relationship between them. Before heading to Chloe's room, she'd unlocked the small safe she had in her room and took a bag of small colored pills from inside. When she entered the girl's room, she was horrified by what she saw in front of her. The girl was squatting in bed, staring blankly and red-eyed. Her hands and face were stained with blood and the white sheet she was sitting on seemed like it came out of a horror movie. Only then Julia had understood the girl's horror, she herself once tried to go against Dalton, but eventually gave in and accepted that she would be better off under his protection. She even fell in love with him and was seriously thinking of starting a family with him. Chloe had to somehow accept what she was being offered was for her own good and stop her stupid attempts at escape. No one escaped Dalton unless they ended up like his brother.

Julia placed a blue pill on the bedside table and said to the girl:

"Look, this pill will make you feel better."

Chloe looked at her with hatred.

"You killed him. You are criminals!" The girl was hoarse.

"Take the pill, Chloe. It will help you forget everything you saw today and make you forget that Andrew died because of you." Julia went to the door and, before leaving, said to the girl,

"I don't want to hear your screams anymore. The girls need to rest."

Chloe was left alone. She reached for the table, took the pill, and swallowed it without thinking, then waited quietly for it to take effect. She was starting to calm down and feel well, but her heart was beating harder. In front of her, there was Andrew, who smiled while telling her they had succeeded. The girl started laughing as he hugged her and whispered in her ear,

"Now sleep peacefully. I'm by your side!" The girl listened to him and closed her eyes, smiling.

Chapter Four

Chloe woke up and looked around scared. She was sweating and had a dull earache.

Her mouth was dry, and she wanted to drink something, but she didn't have the strength to get up. Her eyes stung, and the girl chose to keep them closed to relieve the pain. Then, the door opened, and the girl heard footsteps approaching her bed.

"Do you think I gave her too many pills? Maybe we'd better stop, Julia said loudly."

"No, the shock was too strong for her, and it would be good to overcome it as soon as possible. Next week we must close the deal, and if there is a crisis in the middle of the auction, I will kill her myself." Dalton's words startled the girl, but she preferred to be silent, pretending sleep.

When the door closed behind the two of them, the girl got up and went to the bathroom, where she vomited into the sink. She remembered everything that had happened in the last few days, Andrew's death, his blood on her hands, Dalton and Julia forcing her to take those colorful pills that made her feel euphoric, everything. Her life was a nightmare, and because of her, Andrew had been killed. She stood up and looked in the mirror, but she wasn't able to recognize herself. She had deep dark circles around her eyes, and the traces of the sheet were imprinted on her face. Her hair was tangled, but she remembered that someone had helped her take a shower, probably one of the girls or Julia. She walked back to the bed and reached for the closet, where there was only one pill left. In the last few days, Julia had been taking care to leave them one at a time during her visits. Today she seemed to have forgotten. Chloe sighed irritably and slumped onto the bed.

Towards evening, when she decided that she couldn't wait for Julia to bring her the pill that made her forget, she got up and headed for the shower. She had to make Julia give her more pills. After taking a bath, she put herself together. The yellow of the dress she chose made her skin stand out. She put on her makeup carefully and let her hair fall freely down her back.

She looked in the mirror and was amazed. Julia's lessons were helping her now. She headed for the living room, where all the girls were probably gathered, and although she felt nervous and her body was heavy, she tried to smile when entering.

"Chloe!" Julia greeted her with a fake smile. "I was just about to send someone for you. I thought you fell asleep again!" The woman looked at her with satisfaction.

"I chose my outfit carefully. I didn't want to disappoint you."

"And you did not. The color of the dress makes your eyes stand out. I think I just decided on the dress you will wear next week at the gala." Julia looked at her thoughtfully, and Chloe walked over to the other girls, who were giggling and making signs to each other. Some looked scared. Julia continued to talk,

"Twice a year, we usually organize a gala. It will be phenomenal. You will have the opportunity to meet men and get out of here, as a companion, if they want you. Some of you already know what this is about. We will also have an auction. Everything has to be perfect. Otherwise, Dalton will get angry. Finish eating your fruits, we will then head to the dance hall.

The giggles stopped, and the girls turned their attention to the plates on the table. Some enjoyed them. Others ate out of fear. Chloe ate with hunger and thirst. Her mouth was very dry, and although she'd had enough water, she could not get rid of the thirsty sensation.

When they had finished eating, Julia led the girls to the ballroom. When they finally arrived, she headed for the table where there was a radio and a file.

"Those who are not wearing heels tonight can choose a pair from the corner closet." The woman waited for the girls to put on their shoes, and during this time, she studied the file she was holding in her hands. She then addressed one of the girls.

"Tiffany, do you mind taking a few steps to show the girls what to do when they step on the stage where the auction will take place?"

Tiffany did what she was asked to. She walked straight, making sure to do a slow pirouette from time to time as she looked seductively around her. The girls followed her, and each one of them waved their body provocatively. Chloe tried to do it just like the others and walk with ease, but her body felt heavy and that was making her look like a robot. The girl improvised, smiling, and although she listened to Julia's advice, she felt clumsy. Finally, Julia smiled contentedly and told her that she could stop.

When they finished, Julia urged them to go to the classroom, and the girls did so. When they went out into the hall, Tiffany approached Chloe and whispered so only she could hear,

"I don't understand. How can you be so happy when a man died because of you?" The girl was trapped as the others passed her, some looking at her reproachfully, others with pity. She began to tremble and sweat. When Julia reached her, she could see the anger in her eyes. She reached out and handed her a pill.

"Drink this! You need to stay hydrated!"

The girl took the water bottle from the woman's hand and swallowed the pill, after which she drank all the water. She then followed Julia, and when they arrived, she headed for her desk. She was feeling much better, and her regrets were starting to go away.

"Chloe!" The girl opened her eyes slightly and looked at Julia, who was looking back at her. She had fallen into a state of melancholy. "Show us what you have learned from your past lessons!"

Chloe took the vibrator in her hands and began stroking it with gentle movements. She wrapped her hands around it and tried to do what she had seen in the videos from the previous weeks. The girls whistled and cheered her on, calling her name.

"She says she doesn't know anything about this, but it seems that she is quite good." Charlenne burst out laughing as she looked at her face.

"I think she's made for it!" Tiffany answered the brunette, and they both clapped their hands.

"Enough!" Julia's voice interrupted Chloe, and the girls fell silent, looking innocently at her.

Julia played another movie. After, she started talking, "This is the position called riding. As you have seen, this position gives pleasure to both the man and the woman. In the books I gave you, you will find all kinds of positions, which at some point you will practice. The time is approaching when some of you will leave this place. I tried to prepare you for what will follow, but it's up to you whether the men will pay for you, keep you or send you back. Many of you may not know, but I arrived here in the same way you were brought. I was abducted and sold. And I didn't have anyone to give me advice or to teach me anything. I was beaten up, and when I was brought back to Dalton, I decided to do something for the girls who came in and suffered the same fate I did. I proposed to Dalton to let me take care of the girls who were brought in, and that's how I got to where I am today."

Julia looked at the girls listening to her and was proud of what she was doing for them. They may not have realized it yet, but at some point, they would remember her. She continued to speak, smiling at them.

"You can use everything I have taught you to enter high society where complacency is what matters. You can satisfy a man in such a way as to make him treat you like a queen. It's up to you how far you'll go. But if you think that you will have the same status once you return to this place, you are wrong. Dalton needs money to support you, and you will get this money by having sex with several men in one day. I'm giving you the chance to be more than a luxury prostitute. It depends on you where you end up."

The girls applauded her and thanked her all at once. Chloe laughed and imitated the girls, and although no one noticed her, Julia did not lose sight of her. She said goodbye to the girls and opened the door for them, motioning for the three men, who were waiting outside, to lead them to their rooms.

The big day came, and although the girls seemed to be fine, they were all worried and scared. They were half-dressed in front of Julia, who looked at them proudly. Chloe sat motionless in a chair while another woman was doing her makeup. She felt numb, and her thoughts slid to Andrew; Why did he have to be the one who died?

That morning she had woken up with a strong sense of guilt. She was thinking about Andrew's family and what they would do without him. How would they get out of Dalton's hands? The girl was understanding more and more that she needed to have someone by her side and that the loneliness she had been feeling all her life was killing her inside. Her entire childhood, she'd wanted to know who her parents were, and now she was thinking to who Andrew's child would call Dad. She stood up angrily and left the room, wanting to go back to her room.

"I wouldn't if I were you!" Dalton's voice made her stop abruptly. The man approached her and took her in his arms as he whispered in her ear, "You will return to your chair, where you will wait quietly until you are ready for tonight's party!"

Chloe was trembling from feeling him so close. Dalton looked at her from her head to her feet, his eyes sparkling. He brought his head close to her and kissed her, pressing hard on her lips. Chloe felt paralyzed. Dalton's hands pressed against her jaw, and the girl was forced to open her mouth, allowing him to kiss her with his tongue. The girl felt invaded, but she came out of her state of fear and madly slapped him.

"Fuck you!" she shouted.

Dalton acted quickly, like a panther, grabbing her by her hair and pulling her towards him once more. He was looking her right in the eye as he whispered:

"One day, you'll have to come back here, and I'll be waiting for you. Then there will be no more barriers between us. I will do whatever I want with you!"

"I'd rather die before I get back here! I'll never come back here. You will never put your disgusting hands on me again!"

Dalton began to laugh.

"The kitten pulls out her claws. Very good! Go back and wait for your turn. Now!"

Chloe walked back to the room where all the girls were waiting, and just before she entered, she heard Dalton saying,

"Make sure everything goes well, or Edward will be the one to suffer."

Chloe froze. She felt defeated, her shoulders dropped, and she turned to Dalton with tears in her eyes. The man knew about her little brother and had kept that secret to force her to do as he pleased.

"Please don't do anything to Edward. I'll do whatever you want, just don't hurt him. I beg you!"

The girl was pale and trembling.

"Go back to the room and be ready to get out of here. If everything goes well tonight, I will forget your little secret."

Chloe didn't know how she got back to her chair. She quietly waited until the girls had finished her hair and makeup, then got dressed. She didn't realize how long her thoughts had been with Edward, whom she had sworn she would protect at all costs. She had failed. Her little Edward would suffer the same fate as Andrew.

"Here you go! You will feel better after this." Julia handed her one of the colored pills, which she had in a small bag in her jeans pocket.

"You knew, and you didn't say anything! So, you've waited until now just to make sure I'll do exactly what you want, and you preferred to kill Andrew before threatening me with Edward."

"Andrew deserved it. The fact that he helped you showed us that he was not worthy of our trust. Sooner or later, he would have betrayed us anyway."

"You bastards. One day, I'll take revenge for everything you've done to me. I swear!" Chloe looked at Julia with hatred as the other girls smiled.

"Until you get your revenge, it would be better to do what

you have been taught, so you will see what it means to really suffer."

Julia pushed her hard towards the door the other girls had disappeared through. Chloe followed their footsteps and entered a scene full of blinding lights. When she finally got used to them, she noticed with stupefaction that many men were sitting at tables, watching the girls and observing them carefully. On the wall behind them there were projected photographs taken by Julia a few days before.

Julia's loud voice was heard as she entered the stage. She was dressed in a floor-length red dress. Her dress wrapped beautifully around her perfect breasts, and her hair cascaded down her shoulders. The woman was beautiful and seemed sure of what she was doing. She moved as if she wanted to get all the men's attention on her and her voice was hoarse as she spoke.

"Chloe Turner is twenty-three years old." Julia pulled her hand as she was threatening her with his eyes. "This wonder is over one meter and seventy centi-meters tall with a perfect body, and she is one of our diamonds. The girl is perfectly healthy, and her virtue makes her invaluable. The voices of some men could be heard in the room, but Julia covered them all. "Indeed, the girl is a virgin, and this makes us want a price as high as possible."

Julia pushed the girl in front of everyone, and Chloe closed her eyes, knowing what she had to do. Edward's image haunted her. She began to move, thinking of him, spinning and doing pirouettes exactly as she was expected to. After some moments, Julia made her a sign for her to stop and came closer to her.

Then one of the beasts who had witnessed Andrew's murder approached her and grabbed the girl's hands behind her back as Julia began to tear off the steamy yellow dress that Chloe was wearing. The girl was ashamed and tried to get out of the man's hands to cover herself, but she had no success. Tears filled her eyes, and the men's laughter irritated her.

All she wanted was to get out of there and shoot them all. She could not conceive how all those men there were ready to participate in such sales. The man forced her to show herself, naked, in front of the others, and Julia began to speak:

"We start at 35,000 pounds; I hear a 36,000! 40,000 for the man on the right, 45,000 for the man in the white jacket, 50,000 for the man in the corner, 60,000 for the man in the hat. I hear an 80,000."

There was silence in the room, and Chloe felt lost.

"100,000 pounds!" Chloe looked at the place where the voice came from. There was a tall, black-haired man who had a large scar on his face. His eyes scared her.

"100,000 seems to be the last price. Chloe Turner leaves us for the man in the black cape."

Julia was ecstatic, and Chloe couldn't take her eyes off the man who had paid so much for her. He shook hands with Dalton, who was sitting at the same table. The two were smiling, happy with their deal. There were a few more men sitting at their table: a young man in his thirties, bald and with a lost look, an old man who did not stop smiling flatteringly, showing his golden teeth, with exotic clothing. Behind them, there were several men dressed in suits, probably bodyguards.

There was no time left for Chloe to think about what was going to happen to her. Her nerves were stretched to the limit, and in the following hours, she had to be ready to leave with that mysterious man.

"It would be better if you relaxed. The man who bought you doesn't like naughty women. I advise you to do what he wants!" Julia approached her and tried to calm her down, but the girl was still very nervous.

"Julia, please, let me go! Help me get out of here, and I assure you I won't tell anyone about you." Julia laughed and handed the girl a small red box.

"This is from us. Take a pill when you feel the need. It will help you get through the unpleasant moments. After the first night, I can assure you that everything that follows will please you. So just stop thinking about some way to escape. There is no escape!"

"I'll be back, to finish with you and everything you're doing here. I will destroy you!" Chloe seemed confident in her promises, and although Julia knew the girl was not threatening, she didn't like her hateful gaze. She left the room laughing in an attempt to not show her emotions.

Chloe was taken by one of Dalton's men to the garage, where the one who bought her was talking to Dalton next to a black SUV.

Dalton turned to her and smiled as he stepped towards her.

"She's a real wonder!" Both men looked at her admiringly.

"She really is a rough diamond. The man laughed hoarsely. I knew I could count on you. Thank you so much for what you did! I can't figure out how you always manage to get the most beautiful women."

"The secret of the profession! Dalton laughed, then continued: And don't forget, if you ever get tired of her, let me know and I will take her back."

"It won't be too soon; I can assure you of that!"

The two men winked and shook hands, then Dalton approached Chloe and hugged her.

"I'm waiting for you to come back with my arms open, my little one!" The man let her go and pushed her towards the car.

"Your treasure is ready, Alexander. Enjoy it!"

The girl looked up at the man named Alexander, and she was amazed that one look made her feel so much fear. His black eyes were making her feel uncomfortable. He seemed like a tough, conscienceless man. The girl shuddered and went into the back of the car. She sat in the back, crouched by the window on the left side of the car, watching the road ahead.

The street was full of agitated people. On either side there were shops, restaurants, and street vendors smiling at every passerby. She had never been there before, but she had heard stories. It was a dangerous place where illegal business was done, and no one dared get involved.

They soon arrived at an underwear store. The girl could read above the door the name, Diamond Lingerie. The driver got out of the car, and the girl could see through the window of the store how the salesman gave him a lot of bags. The pill she took before leaving Dalton's building was taking effect, and Chloe was felt calm. She was no longer thinking about anything. She didn't even think to open the door to run away, or to ask for help.

When Alexander hung up the phone, he turned to her and put his hand on her leg. The girl retreated closer to the door, and that gesture seemed to amuse the man who smiled at her, showing his perfect teeth.

"My name is Alexander." The girl looked at the thin scar that stretched from his chin to his ear, and the man continued to talk. Let's forget the conditions in which we've met and try to be friends. He reached for the young woman's leg once more and touched her lightly.

"Let me go, please! I guess you know how I got to Dalton's brothel. Please help me get back home! I have a little brother to take care of!"

The man looked at her for a few seconds without blinking, his right eyebrow raised, which accentuated his scar even more.

"I paid a small fortune for you. I can't let you go so easily."

"I'll give you your money back, I promise, to the last penny."

"I don't need money. You'll soon find out why I chose you. The trip will be long. Rest!"

The man answered the phone that kept ringing, and Chloe closed her eyes, trying to escape from the nightmare she was in. She wanted to forget about everyone. About Dalton, Julia, Alexander, and everything that was going to happen.

Chapter Five

Chloe opened her eyes and looked around. The room was lit by candles on the large table in front of the bed. The bed was huge with white satin sheets and a baldaquin that dropped a fine pink cloth around the bed. She heard footsteps, then saw the door open. The man with the scar on his face and two women entered.

Their whispers made Chloe look at them curiously.

"The girl is beautiful. Looks like Dalton knows your tastes, Honey." The woman who spoke was of pagan beauty, her large eyes coffee-colored and framed by long, thick eyelashes. Her full lips were colored a dark red, and she was dressed in a long black dress with thin straps and a deep neckline. Her black hair was pulled into a tight bun at the top of her head, framing her face with clean skin.

"Yes, Dalton really knows what I like, but what matters is for him to like her."

"He will! Sienna will take care to teach the girl how to behave around him, and we will make sure that everything will go according to the established plan."

Sienna was probably the other girl. She was very beautiful too with blonde hair, long to medium and curly. Her blue eyes and rosy mouth tightened in a thin line made her look like she wasn't satisfied with anything. She was dressed in a pale blue, skater-like dress that reached her knees. She did not speak and looked Chloe right in the eye.

"Leave me alone with her!" The women left the room obediently, and the man approached the bed.

"How are you feeling, little one?"

"I'd feel better if you let me go home."

"I hope you had a good sleep. I don't want you to miss anything while you're here."

"I feel awful. The girl burst into tears. You keep me locked in this room. You make plans and talk about me with other women as if I were not present. Why have you brought me here?"

The man sat down next to her on the bed and pulled the girl closer to him. He lowered his head and touched her lips, kissing her tightly. The act lasted a few seconds, during which the girl struggled to escape. When the man finally let her go, the girl got away immediately.

"You really are more innocent than I thought." The man laughed slightly. "I need you. If you do the right thing, you may be able to redeem your freedom faster than you think."

The girl looked at him in astonishment. Would she be free?

"Tell me, what do I have to do to get out of this hell once and for all?"

"Be the first woman in my brother's life!"

"What?" She asked angrily.

"You know very well why you were brought here, but you didn't know for whom. Everyone thought I bought you for myself, but it's not true. I hope you are not disappointed!" The man was full of pride, and the girl looked at him astonished. He continued: My brother will get married in one month. Sienna is his fiancée. Their fate has been sealed since they were born.

"And what do I have to do with this situation?" Chloe asked, confused.

"My brother has to be prepared for the big day. You see,

103

while the woman must be chaste on the wedding night, the man should know how to satisfy her."

"You mean I must have sex with your brother, who is engaged to Sienna, the girl who has to prepare me for him? Chloe asked, full of disgust. What kind of family are you?"

"Be careful how you talk about my family. The man approached her and slapped her lightly on the face. Our culture is different from yours. Only we can understand it. Sienna was taught since she was a little girl to accept our rules and to obey her man. She will teach you what pleases her husband."

"How old is your brother?"

"He'll be eighteen the night you'll be his woman."

"God! You will use my virginity as a gift for your little brother. How can you be so cruel?"

"I can assure you that we are all aware of this situation. This is our tradition. He is the important one, not you. You'd better not forget that."

"What will happen to me after you offer me to your brother?"

"It depends on your cooperation. If you listen and do what you are asked to, I may offer you the freedom you are asking for. If you refuse to cooperate, you will get sent back to Dalton."

"You may give me my freedom? If I do that, I want you to promise to let me go!"

"Take the role seriously and make sure my brother likes you, and we'll talk about your freedom later."

Chloe watched Alexander turn to the door and walk out of the room.

"Dinner is served in two hours. Sienna will bring you clothes and help you get ready."

"Fuck you!" The man closed the door behind him, letting the

girl scream her anger.

Chloe was overwhelmed. She couldn't believe what was happening. It was a strange situation. She was going to be a man's gift. Better said, a boy who was going to turn eighteen in a few days. And what seemed most unbelievable was the fact that his so-called fiancée would help her be ready for him.

When Sienna entered the room a few hours later, Chloe's eyes were swollen from crying.

"Get up. We have to get ready!" Sienna pulled her by the hand to the bathroom. "Wash your face and apply this cream!" The girl's English was bad, but even so, she managed to make herself understood quite well. Chloe did what she was asked, and when she finished, she stopped and said:

"You're making a big mistake. I was kidnapped and brought here against my will. How can you accept that I will be the first woman in your fiancé's life?"

"You were bought. The girl pulled her even harder. That's how you modern women sell your body without shame."

"You're wrong. I didn't agree to sell my body. I was kidnapped and sold to your brother-in-law. He bought me from the man who kidnapped me without caring how I got there."

The girl seemed to think of what Chloe had said, a few seconds later, she growled,

"Alexander is an honest man who takes care of his family. He decides what is best for all of us."

"If he decides what's best, why doesn't he fuck you instead of his brother and get all of you out of this complicated situation."

Sienna was shocked. She was pale and pulled the hand she had on Chloe's arm as if touching her burned. When Chloe heard the man's voice, she understood why Sienna was looking behind her.

"Looks like you don't want to understand that it's up to you to do what you're told!"

Alexander motioned for the girl to leave and was left alone with Chloe. As he approached her, he spoke harshly,

"I should punish you for the way you've been speaking to Siena. Chloe backed away from him until she hit her back against the wall. Alexander pulled her towards him. The girl tripped and grabbed the man's shirt as she looked at him, scared.

The man grabbed her waist and pressed his body against the girl. He bit her lips, and his brutal kiss was meant to punish her. She tried to move away from him. His hands moved up and down her body, and when he reached her breasts, he squeezed them tightly. The girl moaned in pain and continued to struggle. When the man finally moved away from her, the girl staggered and leaned against the wall. She felt humiliated.

"I'd love to take care of you myself. And if you don't calm down, I'll do it for my brother and find him another whore more willing to satisfy him." Chloe looked at him, scared, and the man began to laugh. Take care to do what you are asked to, or I will have the pleasure of owning this perfect body. Now get dressed into this!"

The man handed the girl a dress, and she took it and went to the bathroom where she put it on. Alexander was behind her and turned her around to close the long zipper that ran from her hip to her neck. He then let his hands caress the girl's arms which began to tremble.

"Me écheis trelaínei[5]! Don't move, agapi mou[6]!"

The man put a chain around her neck with a small teardrop-

---

[5] *you drive me crazy* in Greek.

[6] *my love* in Greek

shaped diamond. You're perfect now. Redo your makeup a little bit. I don't want to see your eyes swollen, and in ten minutes, I want you to be ready. Sienna will be waiting for you at the door to lead you to the living room. Be careful what you say. The girl is not to blame for what's happening to you.

Chloe went to the mirror and looked at herself. Trembling hard, she put her right hand to her swollen lips and tried to hold back the tears that threatened to fall. She had to get out of there, and she had to do it fast. The man insulted her and made her feel insignificant. She put on light makeup, following Julia's lessons, before walking to the door where Sienna was waiting for her, docilely.

With her thoughts lost, the other woman began to walk, and Chloe took advantage of her silence to look around curiously. The hall was long and majestically arranged, along the wall there were several doors. Huge plants were placed next to each imposing pillar, and inlaid eagles were on all the golden benches. The carpet of the same color stretched along the hall, looking very expensive.

The girls walked down the long hall, and Sienna opened the door to a huge living room, a huge, imposing throne table in the middle of the room, and in the middle of it a well-flowing water fountain. The flowers in the room gave off an intoxicating scent.

Footsteps were heard behind them, and the girls turned around in time to see Alexander coming, along with a younger man. Alexander stared at Sienna, who nodded in approval as she smiled at him. Chloe did not understand their sign and continued to look at the young man. He looked like Alexander but was thinner and shorter. His eyes were a rare color, a dark gray with long, slightly curved eyelashes, and he was smiling with full lips. When the two men stopped in front of the girls, the young man took Siena's hand, who had her head down, and kissed her lightly.

"This is Chloe!" Alexander spoke loudly, and his words echoed in the huge room. "Chloe, this is my brother, Ermin."

"Nice to meet you, Chloe!" The young man bent down and kissed the girl's hand, his English was perfect, and his voice was soft.

The girl looked him in the eye and smiled sincerely. The boy looked totally different from his older brother.

"Nice to meet you too!"

"Chloe is a beautiful name! "

The girl looked at Alexander and Sienna, who started a conversation in their language, leaving her practically alone with Ermin. This was probably the plan from the start, but Sienna seemed to be unhappy with something. Chloe moved away from the group a little, but she could see that the young man was always right behind her. When they moved away from a little, she managed to speak:

" My real name is Emily; Chloe is the one they gave me. I don't like it."

"In that case, I'll call you Emily!" The girl smiled slightly at the young man who seemed to want to please her.

"I'd rather you call me like they do! Why are you doing this? You know very well why I was brought here. Why are you behaving so nicely when I'm around?"

The boy grabbed her hand and touched her face lightly as he wiped a tear that was gently dripping on one of her cheeks.

"Just because I know doesn't mean I agree. I know what my brother is trying to prove, but I don't want to be part of all this. You are far too young and far too beautiful to be used this way."

"Sienna will be your wife one day, won't she? Why can't you do it with her, for the first time, like any normal person?"

"Things are far too complicated in my family. I'll tell you everything you want to know one day, but for now, I want you to know that I'm going to try to ruin my brother's plans."

"Can you help me get out of here? I was kidnapped and then sold to your brother." The girl spoke quickly.

"I believe you. Give me some time. I'll think of a way to help you. Until then, we need to make the others believe that their plan is working."

The two went back to the big table, and Sienna looked at them full of jealously, and at the same time, Alexander smiled as he watched them. Ermin pulled the girl's chair out and held it as she sat down, then sat down next to his brother.

The two began to speak in their language, and Alexander did not seem very pleased with what he was hearing from his brother. The girl was tense while looking at them. She was starting to feel like a fool because she has dared to trust Ermin. After all, she had been brought there for him.

"You'd better eat something!" Alexander told her.

The girl was sure that the young man had told his brother everything they had discussed, and that was the reason why Alexander acted so. Sienna was eating quietly and acting like what the two men were discussing did not affect her. Chloe's heart beat faster and faster as she tried to finish eating everything she had on her plate. After drinking some water, she got up and whispered,

"I'd like to go to my room. I feel tired."

Alexander looked at her harshly.

"Sit down. I'll take you there myself when we're all done."

"Where were you born, Chloe?"

She looked at Ermin in amazement. The young man treated her with admiration, and the girl thought that if she had known him in other circumstances, she might have even liked him.

Alexander looked at them suspiciously and was attentive to every word as they continued to have the conversation. The girl thought that the boy probably hadn't told Alexander anything. She began to laugh at the young man's jokes and could not help but smile at Sienna, who was looking at him jealously. Alexander noticed the girl's gesture, and with an angry look, he stood up from the table.

"Are you done, Chloe?" The man asked while waiting for her to get up from the table.

"Actually, I'd love to stay a little longer. I'm glad to talk to your brother."

"I think you'd better stand up. I'm done here!" Alexander cut her short.

The girl listened to him and went after him.

"Next time, try not to act like you were, under the eyes of my future sister-in-law!"

The two were just entering the room, and the girl was walking quietly to the window when she heard the man's offensive words. She turned to him, angry, and shouted:

"To act like what? Like a kidnapped woman and brought here against her will? Like a woman whose rights and life have been forbidden? And in front of whom exactly? You are all criminals! Dalton was a small child next to you." She stopped when she saw that the man was coming towards her full of anger.

"What a whore you are! I told you to behave well, or you won't get along with me. Your life belongs to me."

Chloe started laughing hysterically.

"My life has meant nothing to me since Dalton kidnapped me!"

"I'll show you that life can be much worse than you think if you don't calm down! You better keep that in mind!" The man uttered his last words and then started kissing her, making the girl sigh in pain.

Chloe had no hope of escape. In vain, she tried to escape from the hands that were squeezing her too hard. She was tried hard not to react, but the man's kiss no longer seemed so disgusting. She hadn't been kissed many times, but she could see that the man had experience and although she knew she hated him, he managed to provoke a pleasant sensation.

She put her hands around the man's neck and leaned lightly on him. Alexander abruptly withdrew and pushed her away, and Chloe lost her balance. She hit her head on a massive corner of the bed and lost consciousness. After a while, when she woke up, she was lying in bed, and Sienna was looking at her.

"If you didn't challenge him, nothing would have happened. You're the one to blame for everything!"

Chloe was beginning to remember what had happened before she had fainted. She touched the little bump that came out of her neck and shuddered when she felt pain and dizziness. She pulled her trembling hand back just when Ermin entered the room. Sienna began to speak to him in their own language. He answered carelessly and approached Chloe to the other woman's displeasure.

"How are you feeling? Alexander said you tripped and hit your head on a corner of the bed." The young man was waiting for the girl's confirmation, and she did it at Alexander's threats. "Do you need anything? Alexander says there is no need for doctors, but I am not convinced. You have been unconscious for quite some time."

The boy talked and talked, and Chloe finally smiled trying to convince him that she was feeling well.

"It's time to go." Sienna spoke as she pulled Ermin's arm. "Chloe needs to rest!"

The two walked away, and Chloe was left alone, looking at the large window with bars. She had to get out of there as soon as possible. Sienna was getting more and more jealous. Ermin getting closer and closer. With what was happening between her and Alexander, she didn't exactly know what was going on in her mind. She hated Alexander, but at the same time, she was happy to challenge him.

"Chloe, wake up, Chloe!" The girl opened her eyes to Ermin, who was shaking her lightly. She got up quickly, but her dizziness made her sit back down. The young man helped her stand up and supported her, and then handed her a stack of banknotes.

"Take these. You'll need them. And get dressed into these clothes."

She took the clothes from the young man's hands: a black cape and some trousers and put them on with Ermin's help.

"Where are we going, Ermin?" She asked as she looked at him scared.

"I'll help you get out of here! I know Alexander is the one who caused your accident. My brother is a brute, as far as I'm concerned. He doesn't understand that I'm not gay, and he's stubborn to prove it."

"What? She stopped looking at the young man. It is not a tradition? Alexander told me that it is a custom for men to do this before the wedding and…"

"Chloe, we have to hurry. My brother's men are having dinner. We don't have much time. The situation is much more complicated." The two started walking again. "My brother decided that I have to marry Sienna, but I don't want to, and that makes him think I like men and not women."

"And is it true? Do you like men?"

"No, that's not true. I like women, but my brother doesn't understand that's not the problem. I will never marry Sienna. Our parents made a deal when we were born, but I'm not going to respect it. I want to decide for myself who I will marry, even if my family denies me this right ."

"You're right. You shouldn't marry Sienna just because your family wants you to. They will have to accept that it is your right to choose who you want to share your life with." The girl took his hand and looked at him with sad eyes.

"It's more than that!" The boy sighed, then continued, "We live by traditions, we believe in what has been written for us. Even my brother did what was decided for him years ago, even though he knows he's not happy in his marriage. He is now forcing me to make the same mistake as he did."

They reached a black Range Rover, and Ermin handed the girl the car keys.

"In three minutes, I'll open the gate. Be ready to go out, and don't look back! When you get out onto the street, turn right and then go to the end of the street and you'll see the main road. From there you have to look at the signs and go wherever you want. When you get to the town, park my brother's car somewhere and try to hide. His people will be looking for you for sure.

"Thank you very much, Ermin! One day I will make it up to you, I promise!" The girl said while her tears fell.

"Promise me you'll be fine! That's all I want! I'm sorry you went through all this because of me."

The boy kissed her lightly, then pushed her towards the car. Chloe got into the car, and Ermin disappeared into the dark, rushing to open the gate for her to drive out. After what seemed like an eternity, Chloe noticed the gate opening and started the engine. But then she felt someone put a hand to her mouth, put a gun to her head, and whisper in her ear.

"Keep driving!" Alexander's voice made the girl tremble.

The man took his hand from the girl's mouth but continued to point the gun at her.

"What are you going to do with me? You promised to set me free when it was all over."

"That's only if you would have done your job, my dear, but you preferred to ally with my brother and take me for a fool."

"But you probably heard what interested you. There is no doubt that your brother is not gay. He just isn't in love with Sienna and doesn't want to marry her. You have to respect his right."

"In love or not, my brother will keep his word to Sienna's family. As for you," The man's hoarse voice made the girl shudder, "I'll make sure I didn't pay a fortune in vain!"

"Let me go, please. I promise I'll pay you back to the last pence."

"You'd better save your energy for later! Your tears don't impress me. Stop the car now and move to the passenger seat."

The girl hit the brakes, and the car stopped abruptly. The man swore and waited for the girl to get out of the car, then grabbed her arm and led her to the passenger seat. He then headed for the driver's seat and started the car.

Chloe continued to cry all the way, and when they finally arrived at their destination, she almost fainted from fear. She had a terrible headache. She had been so close to being free, but she felt trapped again because of him.

Alexander held her by the arm as they entered the wooden chalet. He began to speak, as he showed the girl everything, Chloe noticed the phone sitting on a table by the large couch that was in the middle of the living room. There was a small glass table in front of it, on which there were several magazines and a tray of drinks. A velvet carpet covered the wooden floor. The man pushed her to a large mahogany door.

"This is the bedroom." A king-size bed, covered in black satin, occupied most of the room, and the ceiling was made of mirrors.

On one of the walls, there was a closet.

"And this is the bathroom!"

She had seen a bedroom, a living room, and a bathroom, but now she could see that there was also a kitchen. It was long and spacious and had modern equipment. A table with four chairs was nicely placed in the corner. The man was behaving as if she was a guest, not a hostage, and Chloe felt terrified that he would take her to the bedroom and what was to come.

"You can find food in the fridge, and I guess you know how everything works. In the bathroom, you can find a robe on the door, and there are towels in the closet."

The man shrugged and smiled then touched her lightly on the cheek, looking at her pale face.

"Calm down. I won't hurt you!"

"Let me go, please!"

"I can't, the man answered while coming even closer, and then kissed her lightly on the forehead. Don't ask me why. I just can't let you go!"

The girl's sighs intensified, and Alexander hugged her. He took her to the bedroom and made her sit down on the bed before taking off her dress. Chloe was frozen in fear. He suddenly stood up and walked out of the room. When the door closed behind the man, she began to cry and continued like this until she fell asleep.

Chloe woke up alone in the big bed. There was no noise from

115

the other rooms. She got up and walked lightly to the bathroom, where she used the toilet and washed her face. She then put on a set of pajamas taken from one of the closets and opened the bedroom door. The living room and kitchen were empty.

The man seemed to have gone, so she tried to open the windows and doors, looking for a way out, but they were all locked. Then, she remembered the phone she'd seen the night before in the living room and went straight to it and dialed the police.

When the receiver clicked, the girl began to speak like she was out of breath.

"Hello, my name is Chloe. No, my real name is Emily Growdy. I was abducted a few months ago by Christian Dalton and sold to a man named Alexander. The girl was confused as she tried to remember the full name of the person who had bought her."

She remained frozen in fear when she heard a laugh on the other side of the phone, then a familiar voice answered her:

"Alexander Vasiliadis. You really thought I was so stupid as to leave the phone in your hand? Don't underestimate me, agape mou. Calls are forwarded directly to my phone."

"You bastard! I hate you!" Chloe dropped onto the couch, and before hanging up, she heard the man telling her to eat something and that he would soon be back.

The girl threw the phone hard, and it broke when it hit the wall. Then, she stood up again and started looking for a way out of the house. She even tried to unlock the door with a knife. When she saw that it was not possible, she tried the windows. They had bars, and although the girl was able to open them, she could not get through the bars. There was no other house around, and apart from the garden full of perfumed flowers, the girl couldn't see anything. The absolute silence was only interrupted by singing birds.

"Damn you!" She punched the thick window, hurting herself.

She sighed, going back to the couch where she remained, thinking of so many things and of nothing at all at the same time. She just wasn't able to find a way out of that situation. Chloe was starting to doubt more and more that Alexander would let her go. She knew too much about him.

The girl went to the kitchen and prepared herself a coffee with a piece of toast, and although she was not hungry, she knew she had to eat in order to keep her strength. As she ate the bread, she checked the kitchen. There was food everywhere, canned food and ready-to-eat food. The man had the cottage ready for a longer stay, or he had been coming there far too often.

When she finally found a heavy pan with a long handle, she smiled, satisfied. She was looking forward to seeing Alexander again, and so she waited quietly by the living room window and started to come up with a plan.

It was dark outside when she noticed the headlights of a car approaching. Although numb, she hurried to hide behind the door. There was no light in the room, and Chloe wanted to take advantage of that.

A few minutes later, a key was heard in the door lock and the girl was ready to receive Alexander. The man failed to take more than two steps when he was struck on the head with something. Chloe saw him staggering and fall to his knees as he shouted in pain. She quickly went out to the yard and started running, passing by the gate, hurrying to the nearby forest. After a while, she began to lose her breath, and her bare feet were hurting. When she felt something go deep into her right leg, she felt like fainting and stopped, leaning against a tree.

She was starting to feel the cold air from the forest when she heard noises behind her and fell slightly to the ground, near the thick tree. The noise was getting closer and closer, and she was struggling to hold her breath. The footsteps got closer, and although the girl stood up quickly, she could not get too far due to the pain in her feet. The dizziness was getting stronger and stronger, and eventually, the girl was overwhelmed by it.

"Wake up!" A strong voice echoed in the girl's head, and she opened her eyes to Alexander's angry face. "Drink this," the man told her, as he brought her a glass of something gold. She did so and then fell back into her deep sleep. Although her legs stung badly, the hands that cared for her were gentle. Chloe moaned softly and looked at Alexander, wrapping her feet in clean bandages.

"You were a fool when trying to run. Maybe you should know that there is nothing within a ten-kilometers radius around this house. If you try to do that again, don't go barefoot and take the car keys." Alexander was speaking gently to her, but his harsh gaze made her feel guilty. The girl began to cry, and the man took her in his arms and headed for the bedroom.

"I'll prepare you something to eat for dinner. Stay here, be calm, and try to rest."

When the girl was left alone, she hated the weakness she was feeling, wiped away her tears angrily, and promised herself that she would no longer cry in front of that beast who had no mercy for her.

When the man came back, he had a tray full of fruits and food in his hands.

"Eat!" He sat down on the bed and put the tray on his feet.

"I'm not hungry." Chloe protested easily, but the man's

118

words made her regret it.

"I'm starting to get tired of this nonsense. I think we'd better do what I had in mind for you when I brought you here."

"No, please!" Chloe opened her eyes, watching him stand up slowly. "Let me go, please, don't hurt me!"

The man took the tray from the bed and put it down then turned to Chloe.

"If you had listened from the beginning and done exactly what I told you to, maybe I would have set you free. But since I bought you, you've only bothered me." The man quickly caught Chloe. Even though she was trying to get away, she knew there was no way out.

"Willingly or not, you'll be mine, agape mou. I promise you will enjoy it!"

Chloe slapped him hard on the left cheek, and the man squeeze her even harder, making her scream in pain.

"Let me go!"

"If you hit me one more time, you'll regret it bitterly!" Alexander put his body over hers and began to kiss her, making her tremble. Her lips ached from the brutal force with which he kissed her, and she was completely losing her breath. When the man's hand went down to her breasts, the girl tried once more to remove him, but the man's strength was greater than hers.

She stood still staring blankly as the man took off her clothes, kissing her as he did. When the man bit her breasts lightly, the girl screamed, and the man moaned. He also began to take off his clothes. With her eyes closed, Chloe trembled, tired of fighting. Anyway, things would end the way the man wanted. She felt him climbing on her frail body and making a place between her legs.

His hands were everywhere, touching her whole body. When

he penetrated her, Chloe screamed in pain and struggled to free herself. Her tears flowed, and she felt awful. He pushed himself faster and harder into her kissing her with passion. When the man finally moaned loudly and let himself fall on her, the girl felt relieved.

Alexander laid next to her and took her in his arms. She had no energy to resist and the pain between her legs was killing her. She felt dirty and humiliated. She continued to shed her bitterness through tears, and when she finally fell asleep, she felt Alexander climb on her once more.

"No, please, stop it!" She was forced to stay silent by his kiss, and Chloe remained steadfast, without avoiding or straining, while he possessed her body once more.

"I'm sorry, agape mou, but from this moment, you belong to me completely," the man whispered as he put her hands around his neck, encouraging her to participate.

Chloe looked at him disgustingly and replied dryly

"My body may belong to you, but I will never be yours by my own will."

Alexander laughed, then pushed harder into her as he squeezed her breasts in his palms.

"I think you underestimate me, my beautiful! You are completely mine, and at some point, you will give up."

Chloe didn't add anything and let the man play with her unresponsive body until he was tired. The girl breathed a sigh of relief and crouched in a corner until he fell asleep.

"I brought you all the things you left behind when you ran away from my house. I have all of them in the car, and I'll bring everything to you in a few moments. Now I want you to come and tell me 'Good morning' properly. Chloe winced and retreated to the big fridge. Alexander began to laugh hoarsely as he came closer and closer to her.

"Stop it!" The girl trembled. "Wasn't it enough for you to rape me like you did last night?"

The man grabbed her chin lightly and forced her to look him in the eye.

"I only took something that belongs to me, my dear." Alexander kissed her softly and whispered to her, "You belong to me!"

"I hate you!" The girl turned her head disgusted, causing another round of laughter from the man.

"You will learn to love me, agape mou, and you will love me until I get tired of you."

He released her and left the kitchen. Chloe stood against the fridge thinking that she was so dirty because that man used her body as he wished and then held her in his arms all night, without even caring that she was crying.

She headed once more to the small bedroom, where she noticed some of the luggage brought by Alexander. Chloe took the little travel bag where she had all the body and face products, the ones Dalton and Julia had given her as a gift when she left. She emptied her bag until she finally found what she was looking for and smiled.

"If I knew I would bring a smile to your face, I would have brought all these to you sooner."

Chloe winced, and her eyes betrayed the fact that she was terrified. Alexander was taking off his shirt. He lifted her and hugged her.

"How about thanking me properly? "

The man gave her a kiss, and Chloe began to tremble as she put her arms around his neck. The man's tongue came in and out of her mouth as his hands covered her breasts. Chloe sighed, and the man walked away from her, looking at her in disgust.

"Stop crying!"

"I'm not ready yet, please Alexander, my legs still sting terribly!" The girl's words flowed fast, and the man bent down to look at her bleeding legs.

"Why did you get out of bed? The wound's opened again, little fool." The man went to the bathroom, from where he returned with the first aid kit from which he took out a few bottles and a bandage.

Chloe screamed in pain when she felt the fluid dripping on her injured soles. Alexander lightly dabbed the small cuts with one hand, and with the other, he held her leg still. The girl wiped away her tears as she stared at him secretly.

He was a handsome, good-looking man, and those black eyes mesmerized her. Chloe smiled at him as she whispered:

"Thank you!" Alexander smiled at her and pulled her closer.

"Your smile is driving me crazy, agape mou!" The kiss was full of passion, and Chloe was overwhelmed by the pleasant lethargy that was beginning to invade her body. After the man moved away, the girl closed her eyes and breathed a sigh of relief.

"I was going to take a shower, do you want to come with me?"

"But you just put my ointment on my wounds." Chloe quickly made up an excuse, making the man raise his eyebrows.

"You're right. I'll be right back." Alexander went to the bathroom, and Chloe rushed to her things, from where she took out the pillbox. She took one and quickly put it in her mouth, then hid the box under the bed mattress. After this, she laid down on the bed and began to feel her body relax. She was feeling really good. When the man came out of the bathroom with only a towel on, he began to laugh softly.

"Are you okay?" Alexander seemed amused by the girl's condition.

"I've never been better!" Chloe sat down on the bed, unconsciously sensual.

The man's gaze darkened, and he moaned as he watched her. He went straight to her and took her in his arms. The towel slipped, and the girl began to laugh as she walked her hands over his wet body. She pointed her hand at the man's organ, and when she grabbed it, he moaned, then tore the girl's dress. He removed her tiny panties, and as the girl laughed, he turned her face to the sheet and penetrated her from behind.

Chloe kept laughing as the man bit her earlobe. He sprinkled small kisses on her neck, and his hands pulled the girl's hair harder and harder as he penetrated her faster and deeper. Chloe felt good for the first time. Tired of all those sensations, she let him do his thing and closed her eyes. He pushed a few more times, and when he finished, he moaned loudly and then fell on the bed with Chloe in his arms. He continued to hold her in his arms and whispered in her ear,

"You're more than I imagined, agape mou." Chloe turned around and looked him in the eye.

"Then let me go, please, if I mean anything to you!"

Alexander smiled at her and held out his hand to wipe away the tears that fell on her cheeks.

"Because you mean so much to me, I can't let you go! I will be gone for a few days. You will not be locked up, but you will be left alone. Don't worry. Angelo will take care of you and be at your disposal for everything you need. Don't hesitate to ask him if you want something!"

"Am I allowed to leave this house? I feel like I'm suffocating locked up here all the time."

"Of course! Angelo will go with you on your walks, agape mou. But only around this house. Now sleep. In a few hours I'll leave you, and I want to say goodbye to you properly."

The girl felt Alexander reaching for the phone to turn off the alarm, which was ringing like crazy.

The girl did not want him to touch her again. She squeezed her legs as close to her chest as possible, but that only attracted the man's attention.

He began to kiss her lightly on the neck as he was finding his way between the girl's legs. She moaned in pain when the horny man penetrated her.

"No, please, let me go!"

"Calm down, agape mou. You liked it earlier! Stop refusing your pleasures."

"I didn't like it. I hate you, and I'm ashamed of myself because I have to pretend, I like it."

Chloe scratched him as she struggled to escape the man's arms. He got angry, grabbed the girl's hands, and immobilized her as he pushed himself harder and harder inside her. The man finally finished and stood up at the side of the bed. He looked roughly at Chloe. His gaze fell on the reddish marks that he had caused her, then he looked at the tears flowing down the girl's cheeks.

"You will learn to obey me, agape mou, and when you finally do, everything will be different, I promise!"

Chloe saw him walking to the bathroom and heard the water from the shower flowing. She closed her eyes and tried to ignore the noises he was making. When she heard the front door slam, she breathed a sigh of relief. She hated her life and the man who had taken advantage of her body so many times. And she hated Dalton even more for what he had done to her.

She went to the shower and turned on the water. She wanted to erase all the man's caresses, all the kisses he had forced, and all the shame she was feeling when she remembered what had happened last night.

After a while, the water was cold, and her body was freezing, so she stepped out. She went to the kitchen and prepared some coffee, which she drank while looking out the window at the black and bulky car, in which probably was the man meant to guard her.

Finally, she decided to leave the house, and after changing her pajamas into a pair of jeans and a blouse, she came out more determined to get out of all that misery she had let herself fall into. As she was walking outside, she saw a man coming out of the car and start to walk behind her. Chloe continued to walk until her legs hurt. The wounds on her feet had not healed completely.

There were no other house in that area, no people, and the girl could not figure out where she was, but if she had arrived in that place in other circumstances, she was sure she would have liked it. She went back to the house, and as she passed the man waiting quietly by a tree to follow her, she observed him carefully.

He was tall and thin, he had black hair and a sharp face, and his gaze made Chloe tremble. His black eyes looked at her without any emotion, and his sharp mouth did not sketch any expression. He was dressed in a black suit and was wearing sports shoes in the same color. He had a tattoo with the Phi symbol on his neck. As they were walking, the girl saw that the man was limping slightly.

When she entered the house, Chloe headed for the bedroom, from there she took the small box of pills, which she had hidden under the bed mattress, and quickly put one in her mouth. She then went to sit on the living room couch, which was comfortable, and waited there for the pill to take effect.

Edward was smiling from the car and waving happily, but next to him, Dalton and Julia were looking at her with hatred.

"Edward, no!" Chloe tried to reach him, but she could not escape Alexander's hands, who kept telling her:

"You're mine, agape mou, and the boy is theirs. Accept your fate. This is your life now!"

"No!" Chloe struggled to escape from the man's arms, but with tears in her eyes, she saw the black car moving away with the three of them in it. Alexander began to laugh and let her run after them, shouting at her:

"Now it's just the two of us left, my love. I will never leave you."

"Don't let them take Edward. He's all I have! He's mine, let me go with him!"

"Never! You'll only get out of here dead. You hear? Dead!" The man's hands were strangling her while Chloe screamed:

"No!" The girl shouted and tried to free herself from the man's hands.

"Chloe, wake up! Chloe!" The girl opened her eyes and looked at the man wiping her tears, looking at her worriedly. "It was just a dream, my dear!"

Alexander handed her a glass of water, and Chloe emptied it in seconds. She was still scared by her dream, and when Alexander tried to hug her, she avoided him.

"You'd better kill me rather than keeping me locked in here!" Alexander looked at her sadly and touched her trembling lips.

"Angelo told me you didn't really touch the food while I was gone."

"I wasn't hungry. Can you blame me?" She said while trying to get up from the couch, but the dizziness gripped her, and she began to tremble. Alexander caught her just before falling.

"I think you'd better go to bed, agape mou. I'll cook something for you." The man took her in his arms and headed to the bedroom where he put her in a chair, then changed the bedsheets and packed away the clothes that had been thrown everywhere in the room. When he finished, he helped her to go to bed and wrapped her in a white, fluffy blanket.

He looked at her for a few moments before leaving the room. She was so young and so lost, and her eyes full of hurt and disappointment were breaking his heart. He kept telling himself that one day she would understand that next to him, she had security and protection.

He left the room, and when he returned, he had a round box in his hands, which he carefully placed on the bed next to Chloe.

"This is for you. Open it when you feel ready. I think you'll like it!" Chloe continued to look blankly, and when the man left the room, she pushed the gift away with disgust. She didn't need the man's presents. All she wanted was to die. Alexander returned and would probably soon come to her. To the bed where he thought he had every right to do what he wanted with her body.

"Where did you get these?" Alexander came in angrily.

The girl pulled the blanket over her head, making the man's gift box fly to the other side of the room.

"I asked you something! Where did you get these drugs from?"

"Give them back to me. They're mine!"

"Do you have any idea what these are? You're stupid. I'm not surprised you didn't eat anything the other day or why you've been sleeping all the time over the last few days.

Chloe rushed to take the pills from the man's hand, but Alexander acted faster and grabbed her hand tightly, making her moan in pain. He then pushed her and headed for the bathroom, where he emptied the contents of the box into the toilet, then flushed.

"You bastard, why did you do that? They were mine! You had no right to do that!" Chloe began hitting his chest, and the man pushed her hard against the wall.

"Drugs, they were drugs. Ecstasy, to be more precise. It causes addiction, and although for the moment they make you feel good, after the effect passes, they knock you down. Angelo got them for you, didn't he? Answer, you little idiot! Tell me what you gave him in return? You sold yourself for some drugs?"

Chloe was terrified as she listened to Alexander, who doubted his man. Andrew's face came to her mind, and the girl began to tremble when she remembered how he died.

"No, it wasn't him! How can you not trust your man?"

"I have do not doubt him, agape mou!" Alexander measured her with disgust and desire at the same time. "I just don't trust you!" The man left, and Chloe headed for the living room, angry. He had guts, no joke! Before leaving the room, the girl heard a whimper and looked at the box, which Alexander brought her. She took it and looked at what was in it. A small ball of white fur looked at her, scared with his big black eyes. Chloe took him in her arms and hugged him tightly to her chest. She headed for the kitchen with him, where Alexander was talking to Angelo.

"Julia gave them to me!" The two men looked at her, one angry and the other relieved. "She used to give me a pill to make me forget that Dalton killed his brother in front of me. You see, the man died because of me. He tried to help me get out of that hell, but we were caught, and he was shot in the head by Dalton.

Then, they continued to give me drugs just to make me do what they wanted. Before leaving them, they gave me this box and told me it was their gift."

Alexander told Angelo to leave and went closer to the girl. He hugged her, but Chloe backed away, showing that she had the puppy in her arms.

"Thank you for this gift! It's awesome!

"I thought it would be good for you to have company while I am gone. Have you thought about what you will name it?"

Chloe thought for a few seconds, then lit up her face and whispered,

"Hope!" Alexander touched the puppy and leaned over to Chloe, kissing her on the forehead.

"A very nice name. Go to bed now. You need to rest. I'll prepare some food for both of us and our little Hope." Chloe did so, and when she got to the bedroom, she sat down on the bed with Hope sleeping peacefully next to her. The current situation was disgusting to her, but Alexander seemed to care about her. Maybe one day, she would persuade him into letting her see her little brother.

That evening, Alexander and Chloe had their dinner by candlelight. The girl listened to him talk about his childhood, about his parents, who had died in a car accident, leaving the two children in the care of his grandfather, who was a tough man. He had taught them the Greek traditions, which the two brothers had been followed all their lives. After his grandfather's death, Alexander was the one who came to run the family's business. He was also taking care of the whole family, and hence, he was the one who was making all the important decisions for everyone. Before he died, the old man asked him to promise him that he would keep his promises and that they would marry their promised women.

After dinner, the two moved into the living room, where they drank the tea Alexander had already prepared. The girl took a mouthful and grimaced, then put the cup away, but Alexander insisted on her finishing it, telling her that it would do her good after all the drugs she had been consuming. The girl listened to him and drank all of it. The tea was reddish, with a blackish tinge and a little bit of a sour taste.

"Tell me about yourself!"

Chloe was looking at Alexander while he was looking at her through the curtain of eyelashes, and as she analyzed him, she thought that he was not an ugly man. He was very handsome, and his eyes mesmerized her.

"I can't say much about myself. I grew up in an orphanage. I never met my biological parents, but I was lucky to come across a woman who took care of me and helped me get a good education and made sure to keep me out of trouble."

"I think it was tough for you, agape mou!"

The man took the cup from her hand, put it on the table, and then massage her feet.

"Is that woman still alive? Is there someone else that you were close to when you lived there?"

Chloe looked at him and decided at the time that he deserved her trust. The man, although a stranger holding her captive, was not like Dalton. Earlier, he had chosen to trust her, and he believed her when he told her that Julia was the one who gave her the drugs.

"There's someone. His name is Edward! The man frowned and looked at her harshly. I promised him that when he would leave the orphanage, he would come to live with me."

"What relation do you have?" Alexander asked her, attentive

to the girl's reactions.

"The day I found him abandoned at the orphanage door, I decided that I would protect him and give him the love I never had. And I did until Dalton decided to kidnap me. He is my little brother, Alexander, the little brother who is once again alone in the world," said the girl bursting into tears. "I promised him that I would take care of him and that I would wait for him to leave the orphanage and that we would live together as a family. And I disappointed him!"

"You didn't choose to leave him. You were forced to do it. I'm sure he'll understand when you tell him."

Alexander leaned over and began to kiss her. He began to caress her breasts with slow movements, and when Chloe moaned, he pulled her on the soft carpet by the couch. The girl felt excited, and although she knew she did not want to have sex with the man, she gave in to the sensations.

She began to kiss him back, and when he began to take off his clothes, the girl leaned lightly on the carpet in a pleasant lethargy. She felt his hands pull at her pajamas. He reached for her black lace panties as he climbed on her body. He removed them and began to caress her between her legs. When the man replaced his hand with his mouth and began to kiss her deeper and deeper, the girl moaned deeply and was overwhelmed by the thousands of sensations she was feeling in her body.

Chloe reached out to the man's head and grabbed his hair, then began to push him. The man laughed hoarsely and, laying down on her, made himself room between the girl's legs and penetrated her slowly. Chloe raked her nails down his back and began to moan more and more often, joining the moans of the man, who let himself fall on her.

Chloe didn't realize what was happening to her, and

although her mind told her to control herself, her horny body began to light up again. She reached out to Alexander and began to caress his chest. He opened his eyes and led his hand to her mouth, and she bit his fingers slightly. Chloe gasped lightly from pleasure and, with her other hand, touched the man's penis.

The girl began to explore it and noticed how it was getting harder and bigger. She remembered Julia's lessons, brought her mouth closer to him, and began to suck lightly while licking it. Alexander pulled her hair and got up, pulling her after him. He pushed her to the bathroom, and when he reached the bathroom, he turned her face to the mirror. He began to kiss her neck and caress her breasts as he pressed against her ass. Chloe looked in the mirror and didn't recognize herself. She looked wild with ruffled hair, blushing cheeks, and her red lips making sounds of pleasure. She looked carelessly at her breasts in the man's hands and at how he was playing with her nipples.

"I want you to see the wonderful sensations that you cause me, agape mou!" The man's whispers disturbed her, and although she wanted to stop everything, her body was not listening to her. Alexander lifted her and penetrated her while the girl clung tightly to the sides of the sink.

"Open your eyes, my love!"

Chloe listened to him and looked him in the eye. The man continued to push himself into her and moan. He had drops of sweat on his forehead, and he took one of his hands to the bud between the girl's legs and began to caress it with circular and slow movements. They both started screaming with pleasure as Alexander was penetrating her harder and harder and they both reached orgasm simultaneously.

When they finished, Chloe let herself fall into the man's arms. The tired woman was taken to bed, where she fell asleep in the man's arms.

"What did you put in my drink last night?" Chloe asked while entering the kitchen, where Alexander was preparing something to eat for breakfast.

She was angry and feeling ashamed because she remembered what had happened last night. The man smiled at her and asked her to sit down on the chair.

"Good morning to you too. I hope you had a good sleep! I slept like a baby."

Alexander placed two plates filled with scrambled eggs, bacon, mushrooms, and toast on the table, and next to each plate, there was a coffee and a glass of orange juice. Chloe watched Alexander, who was behaving as if the whole situation was normal.

"I wasn't behaving normally last night. You had to put something in my drink!" Chloe had a red face because of the shame.

"Why don't you just accept that you liked what happened last night?" said the man grabbing her hand and kissing her.

Chloe shuddered and tried to withdraw her hand, but Alexander held her tightly. "You felt pleasure that we both loved, agape mou. You can't deny what we feel when we are together. We are meant for each other."

"Never! You're no better than Julia. She was drugging me because she wanted me to be unaware of myself. You do it to take advantage of me."

Chloe got up and walked out of the kitchen, but Alexander was faster and pulled her next to him.

"Never compare me to that bitch again!" Alexander kissed her angrily.

When the kiss became gentler, the girl's legs softened, and

pleasant sensations began to possess her entire body. Alexander stopped and, as he looked her in the eye, wiped the traces of saliva from his full lips.

"You can deny it as much as you want agape mou, but your body knows that you belong to me. It's a matter of time before you give up completely. Now let's finish breakfast. After this, I will leave, I will not be away for more than a few days, but I will reward you on my return."

Alexander kissed her once more, then pushed her to the table. Chloe sat down and began to eat quietly. She hated that man and knew he was using her to meet his own needs, and even though he knew she was there against her will, he didn't want to release her. She would never forgive him for holding her captive, and even if she was feeling desire for him and feeling good in his arms, she would never give him the satisfaction of knowing that.

A noise was heard from the door, and the girl remembered the little puppy. She stood up and opened the door, then looked at Hope running and playing beside Alexander's feet. Her food was in the bottom drawer. Alexander pointed to it, and Chloe headed for the dog's food. She took out the new bowls, along with the puppy's food, then filled them. The puppy began to eat, and Chloe caressed her lightly on the back. Then she looked at Alexander, who was looking at her gently and said,

"Thank you!"

The man pulled her towards him and hugged her.

"I really like you, Chloe! More than you can imagine! Please give me a chance before I let you go."

"I can't accept what's going on!"

"And yet here you could have everything you want. You have security and protection. The man kissed her slowly. Understand, agape mou, I just want you to be happy, and I promise I'll do everything in my power to make this happen."

"I need freedom. Let me go to Edward. I need him, and he needs me."

"I promise we'll discuss all this situation on my return! Now let's say goodbye properly."

Alexander led her to the bedroom, where he undressed her lightly, and Chloe was overwhelmed by pleasant feelings.

Chapter Six

Chloe was on her way home with little Hope when she noticed the luxury black car heading for the chalet. It was supposed to be Alexander, she wasn't expecting anyone else to visit her and Angelo was at the store. The girl had asked him to buy her some things as the fridge was almost empty, and Alexander had yet to come back. It had been a week since he left. He had only called her once to make sure she had everything she needed and to tell her he was missing her. Chloe didn't know what to think about him. She felt good when he was around, and if they had met in different circumstances, she might have come to care for him.

When the car stopped, Chloe looked inside and began to tremble. She took the puppy in her arms and ran inside. She was ready to close the door when it was pushed hard and slammed against the wall. Dalton smiled at her from behind the sunglasses he was wearing.

"Morning, Sunshine! Who thought we'd see each other so soon?" The man approached her, and Chloe lost consciousness. When she recovered, the girl heard the man talking to a woman. Their voices were filling the room.

"Wake her up! We don't have time for this now. The man who's guarding her could return at any time." Chloe opened her eyes and looked astounded at the beautiful brunette who was next to Dalton. She was looking back at her with hatred and began to talk to her.

"I can't let my husband have everything he wants anytime he feels like it. Especially now that we're going to have a baby. He has to stop !"

The woman was touching her belly, which was slightly swollen, and Emily rolled her eyes when she realized who the woman was.

"Alexander!"

"He probably forgot to mention that he probably forget to remind you that I am still his wife or that we will soon have a child."

The woman continued to speak harshly to her, "You see, my dear, Alexander likes to keep himself busy. This house is intended to fill his void. I hope you didn't think you were the only woman whom he has brought here. There were a few more before you, but he always comes back to me when he gets bored of the ones like you. It's different with you. I saw the way he was looking at you when he brought you home. And even though you were for his brother, he was far too interested in you. I can't afford this, and that's why I called Dalton. He's helped me with such things before."

"Don't let him take me back, please! I promise you'll never hear from me again if you let me go. Chloe grabbed the woman by one of her hands and pulled on her with despair. Please help me!"

The woman pulled her hand back and replied bluntly,

"Alexander is my husband. I can't let you take him away from me. You may feel that he loves you, but it is not true. I am the only one he cares about. He is only using you! "

Chloe looked at the woman who was jealous and kept throwing harsh words at her.

"And yet you are here, insecure and scared. You know very

well that Alexander prefers to spend time with me." Chloe was nervous, and although she knew she was challenging the woman with her words, she continued to scream, "You went behind Alexander's back, and I can't help but wonder how he will react when he finds out the truth? Before he left, he told me that he loved me as he had never loved anyone in his life. I'm sure he'll kill you and Dalton."

The woman slapped Chloe hard on the face, and the girl pounced on Leila, but Dalton caught her and tied her hands behind her back, then headed for the exit.

"I'll take care of her from now on, Leila!"

Dalton stopped when the woman leaned in front of them and reached out, showing a box of tea to Chloe. The girl looked at the tea box carefully and asked herself why Leila was showing her the box of tea she used to drink before bed? The woman laughed ironically as she started saying:

"If he would have loved you so much, he wouldn't make you drink this tea. It is called khat, and it's used to stimulate the desire to have sex. I bet he gave you a cup every time he fucked you."

Chloe was shocked when she realized that what the woman was saying was true. She had no desire to have sex with Alexander. It was the effect of the tea he was making her drink every time.

"Damn you and Alexander!" Chloe started screaming. "You're both just as miserable! I hope you rot in hell!"

Dalton answered the phone that kept ringing and, after he hung up, continued to pull Chloe to the door.

"Enough! Our man confirmed that Alexander's bodyguard is heading to the chalet. We need to hurry."

Chloe tried to stall, resisting when the man pulled her to the car, but Dalton caught her hands behind her and handcuffed her, then he put a handkerchief in her mouth. Chloe struggled and screamed without any success as the man slammed her into the back seat of the car. Dalton led the brunette to her red car, which was parked behind the black one. Chloe saw in the rearview mirror how the man kissed Leila on the cheek, held her door open, and then closed it after she got inside.

When he returned, he climbed to the driver's seat, then started the engine. Dalton drove carefully and from time to time looked at her and smiled or winked. The road was long, and Chloe felt her mouth dry from trying to scream every time the car stopped at a crossing. The girl was terrified that she had to return to that place and that Dalton would keep the promises he had made before selling her to Alexander.

When they arrived in the town, it was already dark, and the girl looked sadly at all the tall buildings. She has always imagined how little Edwards will go to school here. Her heart was broken, and her last hope of escape had died when Dalton appeared that morning. The girl began to struggle when she realized where they are going, and that attracted Dalton's cunning gaze. '

"Welcome home, my Sun!"

The street they next entered was very agitated. Different kind of restaurants were there, coffee shops, and small colorful stores in bright red, yellow, or orange colors. The street was full of this type of builings. On the small brothels on that street had in their shop windows women dresses in short, red satin dresses with black flowers embroided on them.

Dalton stopped the car in front of a small grocery store and went in. When he came out, he was holding a black cape. He tried to pull Chloe out of the car, and the girl took advantage and kicked

139

him in the abdomen. Dalton whistled and grabbed her hair as he pulled her hard out of the car. As he put the cape on her shoulders, he whispered in her ear,

"You'd better not piss me off tonight. I'm too tired, and if you force me to correct you, it may not end well for you."

Chloe swallowed hard and let herself be led by Dalton down the dark path between the houses and the heavily lit casino. The man opened a door and pushed Chloe down the steps leading to the basement where Andrew had been killed. Nothing seemed to have changed, but Chloe felt the danger behind the silence. Finally, they arrived at the dining room, and Dalton took her gag out of her mouth, then removed the handcuffs as well. He then headed to the small table where he kept the alcohol bottles and opened one of the wine bottles. After pouring wine into two glasses, he handed one of them to the girl, who touched her wounded wrists. Chloe took the glass and drank lightly. She was thirsty and did not want to provoke Dalton.

"Welcome back!" Chloe looked at him anxiously. She didn't know what to expect from him.

"Where's Julia?" she asked him hoarsely.

Dalton began to laugh and toasted with the girl's glass.

"Julia had a minor accident in Florida." The man kept quiet for a few seconds, keeping Chloe in suspense, then kept talking. We decided to parachute, and the one she used to have some technical issues. Unfortunately, her parachute did not open. Before jumping, she started crying and begging me to go back, but I was determined to parachute. The man laughed at what he was telling.

"You killed her!" Chloe trembled as she realized that what the man was saying was true.

Dalton came closer to her and leaned over, then licked her

wine-flavored lips. Chloe took a few steps back.

"She was getting too dull, and she was bothering me too much," Dalton said while coming closer and closer. "Julia was a control freak, she wanted me to herself, and maybe it would have worked if she hadn't bothered me so much to please her. Seriously, the woman had become very dull.

When Chloe had nowhere to retreat, Dalton took advantage and forced her to stay there, sitting between her and the door. "When Leila called me and asked for help to get rid of a problem, I imagined all sorts of things, I had all kinds of ideas, and although I knew that you would come back to me one day, I didn't expect it would be so soon. You are the right person at the right time!"

"The right time? What do you mean by that?" Chloe was trembling with all her body.

"I want you to take Julia's place!"

"Never!" The girl was pale and looking for a way out.

"I think you should think again. Dalton grabbed her by her arms and pulled her hard towards him." Chloe began to struggle, which made Dalton grin and draw her closer to him. He then kissed her, and although the girl tried to get out of his hands, she did not have the necessary strength. In vain, she asked him to leave her alone. Her prayers and tears, along with her attempts to escape, seemed to excite Dalton even more.

He slammed her without any mercy on the massive wooden table, then began to tear off her clothes. Chloe began to struggle harder when her blouse tore. Dalton hit her hard across her mouth. The girl hit the table hard. Blood spread all over her face.

She continued to struggle and resist the man. The man's touches were harsh and painful, she had a lost look with tearful eyes and a bleeding mouth. Chloe would have given anything to get rid of him and his hands.

When the man penetrated her, the girl remained motionless. She no longer felt the pain. Something inside her was dying. The man began to slap her in the face, and although she felt the blows, Chloe no longer defended herself. Dalton pushed harder and harder into her, and when he finished, he got up and closed his pants, satisfied with himself.

"You'd better think about my proposal. I assure you that it would be much better for you to accept me than have this treatment from other men."

Dalton walked to the door and left the room. Chloe slid to the floor and cried until her tears dried.

When the door opened, a tall man entered the room, and the girl was frightened when seeing him coming towards her.

"Leave me alone, please! Don't touch me!" Her voice sounded was hoarse and the girl tried to cover her sore breasts without much success.

The man picked her up from the floor and left the room with her in his arms. Chloe kept her eyes closed and asked to be left alone. When she was put down, the girl opened her eyes and saw the man closing the door behind him. She looked around and soon realized that she was in her old room. She tried to get up, but her whole body ached.

In her attempts to stand up, she fell out of bed carelessly. The girl decided to crawl to the small bathroom where she started the shower and remained under the water. Eventually, she got out of the shower and put on her robe, then collapsed into the big bed that smelled of cheap perfume.

The night passed and the girl thought of how to escape. Taking Julia's place was not a possibility. She could never force other girls to go through what she went through herself. She would never do it, and if she had to kill Dalton to escape that hell, she would. She would start with him, then take revenge on Alexander and his wife.

Chloe fell asleep in the morning. It had been a very long night for her, during which she had imagined various ways to make Dalton pay for everything he had done to her. When she opened her eyes the next morning, she felt swollen from crying incessantly. She wanted to believe that she was in a nightmare, but the room and her body confirmed that what had happened the night before. The door opened, and Dalton entered the room.

"Good morning, Sunshine!"

Dalton smiled as the girl took a few steps back, clinging to the wall behind her. The two looked at each other, one with hatred, the other with pleasure. Eventually, Dalton was the one who broke the silence. "Have you thought about my proposal?" The man began to pull the sheet that covered the girl's body.

"Never!" she said hoarsely, and her voice made Dalton stop abruptly.

"What did you say?"

"I'll never take Julia's place." Chloe looked at him with hatred and continued to speak; "I will never be able to accept being the executioner of innocent girls."

"Very well!"

The man walked to the door and opened it and the man from the other evening appeared and Chloe started to tremble when seeing him. He didn't look more than thirty-five years old. His imposing height and robust body scared her. The man was dressed in a dark suit and had colorful sneakers on his feet. His white skin contrasted with the color of his clothes, making him look pale, and his small blue eyes could make anybody want to hide under the bed. He seemed like a dangerous man and just looking at him, you could have felt threatened. Chloe began to tremble while trying not to look at him.

"Marek, I want you to take her to one of the empty shop windows. Undress her and tie her to the bed."

"Yes, sir! The giant turned to Chloe and caught her in his big arms. Chloe tried to get out of his hands, but without success. They left the room, and Chloe's screams could be heard in the hallway leading to the elevator. Dalton followed them. He seemed angry, and before leaving he told the man,

"Make sure she's busy all day." He walked away. When they were left alone, she whispered to the giant:

"Why are you doing this?"

The man did not answer and did not make any sound. The girl began to struggle harder and continued screaming. She thought maybe the man was deaf, but he seemed to understand everything when Dalton had spoken to him. She had to make him talk somehow.

"Let me go, please, help me get out of here! Dalton is a bastard. He kidnapped me!"

The two arrived in a hallway lit by some colored LEDs in a dark red. When the man stopped at door number four, Chloe began to cry helplessly. She was put on the bed dressed in red satin, undressed against her will, and tied with leather straps to the bedposts. The girl struggled to get away from the man.

"Leave me, don't touch me!" Tears flowed down her cheeks as she begged Marek to leave her alone.

Marek tore a piece of material from her blouse and put it in her mouth, then left the room. The girl breathed a sigh of relief when the man left the room without touching her. She looked at the hall through the large window and saw several men looking at her, and she began to tremble when one of them headed for

Marek.

When the door opened, and the man entered the room, Chloe began to struggle again. The girl begged him not to touch her. The man headed for the closet next to the bed and pulled out a small leather whip from one of its shelves. He began to hit her lightly on the breasts, advancing towards the girl's feet, while the men left outside were laughing at them.

Chloe tried to speak, but the piece of cloth in her mouth wasn't allowing her to say what she wanted to. Her body stung from the whip lashes. When the man finally stopped hitting her, he headed for the window and pulled the blinds, then began to take off his pants.

When naked, he took a condom from the same closet and put it on, looking at Chloe with desire. He then climbed on her and began licking her shoulders, neck, and breasts. His robust body crushed the girl's and Chloe closed her eyes, praying that everything would end quickly.

When he penetrated her, the girl felt a burst of pain. The man was pleased to see her in pain. As he pushed into her harder he slapped her from time to time with his whip over her red breasts. The man finished and let himself fall on her, breathing hard. After a few minutes, he stood up, and while watching his expensive watch, he began to get dressed.

Chloe looked at him with hatred. His black hair was thick, and he had a mustache and a robust, hunched body. The man was about fifty years old. His eyes, a soft brown, were looking at her, smiling. Before he left, he took out his wallet, from where he took a banknote and threw it at the girl.

"It was a real pleasure!" His voice echoed in the girl's head for a long time after he left the room. It was a sharp voice that repulsed her.

After a few moments, another man came in, then another, and at one point, Chloe stopped hoping it would stop. She remained inert. Her mind was empty, her body without feeling. She was disgusted with herself. At one point, she lost track of the men who visited her and fainted from exhaustion.

When she woke up, she was in her room and heard the shower flowing. Marek came to her and picked her up, heading with her to the bathroom. Chloe didn't say a word. She couldn't scream or argue. She wasn't even praying. She was exhausted both physically and mentally. The man put her in the shower, washed her gently, then wiped her and tucked her into bed.

The next day she was taken to the same room and visited by other men, who were more and more lustful and perverted. Chloe kept her eyes on the ceiling all the time and tried to disconnect, without success. She felt all the caresses, all the blows. She heard all the moans and indecent words.

When Dalton's man took her to the shower, he noticed that the girl was bleeding. He continued to treat her gently and, after bringing her back to her bed, treated her with cream and forced her to eat the hot soup he had brought, then gave her a pill. Before leaving the room, he raised the girl's head and looking her in the eyes, whispered to her:

"You'd better accept Dalton's proposal, or this won't end well. He left, and Chloe closed her eyes, tired.

When she opened her eyes, frightened by the ironic laughter in the room, she saw Dalton, who was laughing as he watched her.

"It doesn't seem like you enjoyed the treatment." He moved next to her and gently touched the corner of her mouth.

"Two days have been enough to make you accept my proposal?"

Chloe didn't say a word and closed her eyes again, refusing to look at him. The man got angry and slapped her face. Chloe shuddered but continued to remain silent, and that made Dalton, who continued to hit her, even angrier.

The girl's tears pleased the man, and when Chloe tried to avoid his hands, he threw himself at her and began to take off her clothes. He was drunk and excited, and he tore her nightgown and continued to hit her hard for the next few hours, fucking her like crazy. Before fainting, the girl noticed his mad look and the excitement caused by her pain.

Chloe stayed in bed for a few days. After Dalton visited her that night, she was no longer taken to the window shop. The only one who came to her room was Marek, who helped her take a shower, eat, and apply some cream to the wounds caused by Dalton. The girl let him help her, and although she did not speak to him, she caught him looking at her with pity from time to time. She heard his words in her head, whispering: *'Accept Dalton's proposal!'* She was exhausted, and as soon as she put her head on the pillow, she fell asleep.

When she began to feel better, Chloe thought about what she had to do. She hated Dalton, and every time she thought about him, she promised herself that one day she would kill him. She hated everything around her. She hated her body. She hated her life.

Not even the thought of her little brother was brightening her anymore. She was aware that she would never see him again, and she was also aware that she would not escape that living nightmare. And it was all because of Dalton.

When she finally accepted the situation, she accepted that she had to take Julia's place. If not for her, for the girls in that brothel. And if she died, she would do it while trying to get

Dalton to pay for everything he'd done.

"Get up!" Chloe looked at Marek, who'd entered the room without making a noise. "Dalton wants to see you."

Chloe winced when she heard the name of the man. Her body was still sore. The girl stood up slightly but got dizzy and fell. Marek grabbed her arms. She laid in bed while trying to clean up the chaos in her mind. She had failed, but she was more and more determined to get rid of Dalton.

"Put yourself together. Dalton doesn't like to see his women like this. At least that's what Julia should have taught you."

Marek's voice was harsh, and Chloe headed for the bathroom, where she looked in the mirror. Her hair was a mess, and black circles surrounded her eyes. The girl tried to stop shaking and finally managed to get ready. She dressed in a light dress, which she found in the closet. When she found nothing but heeled shoes, she decided to go barefoot. She wasn't going to show off in front of Dalton. If she accepted his game, she wanted to do it her way.

When she reached the living room door, where Dalton was waiting for her, Marek leaned over to open the door and whispered in her ear:

"If you don't accept his proposal, you'll return to the window shop."

Chloe closed her eyes, disgusted by the images that came to her mind. When she opened them, the door was open, and Dalton was waiting for her. He grabbed her chin and studied her appearance for a few seconds before saying:

"I'm glad to see I didn't hurt you as much as I thought. I'm sorry, my love, I'm losing my temper too quickly."

"You are sick!" She whispered and her eyes sparkled when seeing Dalton turning to her, but she kept talking, "You want to take everything by force. You like to cause pain. You have serious problems with self-control. But you will not touch me…"

"Or what?" Dalton approached her, laughing, and looked at her provocatively.

The girl took a few steps back and replied,

"Damn you! I accept your proposal, but that is my condition. You will not touch me again…"

Dalton looked at her for a few seconds, not letting anything be read in his eyes, then nodded. He returned to the table and pulled out a chair as he indicated for her to sit down. He then showed her the coffee machine on the table next to the TV.

"As far as I can remember, you drink sugar-free coffee with no milk?"

"Yes, thank you!" Dalton pressed the coffee maker button and waited until the cup was filled with coffee, then put it on a plate, along with a teaspoon, which he then placed on the table in front of the girl. He began to speak as he sat in front of the girl on the opposite side of the table.

"I am willing to accept your offer if you promise me that you will not try to run. You have to understand that you will have more freedom if we make this pact, and I don't want to always be worrying that maybe you'll try to run. After a while, if business continues to go just as well, I'll let you get out of here."

"You mean, you'll get rid of me, the same way you got rid of Julia?"

Dalton began to laugh and continued to speak,

"Julia wanted it, and you have a point in your favor, I have to admit. However, I don't think you'll start making plans for the future with me. Not when I know how much you hate me. And as long as you do your job well, I won't mind. As for the promise not to run away from here, you'd better keep your word.

Remember, I know your little secret, and wherever you'll try to hide, I will find you!"

Chloe winced, and the cup fell out of her hand.

Dalton handed her a napkin, and the girl tried to wipe the spilled coffee.

"No!"

"Exactly! Your little brother, Edward? You have no idea how much money I can make with him. I have been thinking about this for a while now, but I have to solve the problem with the girls."

"Don't do it, please! Chloe got up. Don't touch Edward, and I'll do what you want."

Dalton walked around the table, and when he reached Chloe, he looked at her, satisfied with himself.

"I'm sure you'll be obedient." He kissed her loudly on the lips, then returned to his place. "As for the touching part, there will come a day when you will come into my bed alone. Until then, I guarantee you that I will not make you mine against your will, as long as you take care to keep the girls under control. Since Julia is no longer in charge, it's like they've gone crazy."

Chloe refrained from contradicting him, looked down, and swallowed hard. The man was a psychopath. She had to be very careful with him. She finally understood that the more she resisted, the more she grew his desire to make her obey.

"Very well, I will help you with them."

"Let's get some work done now. I wasted a lot of valuable time trying to convince you of what I already knew was going to happen." The man opened a file and began talking to the girl about her duties.

Chloe entered the gym in the middle of a fight.

"You may be happy to be here, but we are not!"

"You are right! I like it. At least here, I have a roof over my head, and I have something to eat. We should all be grateful for what Dalton is offering us."

Tiffany was arguing with one of the new girls, a brunette woman

"You see things differently because you chose to be here. I was kidnapped instead. Kidnapped! My mother is looking for me. I'm sure everyone is suffering because they don't know anything about me. I never wanted to be a prostitute like you!" The girl was cried hysterically, and Tiffany slapped her hard.

"Enough!" Chloe said bluntly and approached the girls.

She grabbed Tiffany's hand and pushed her hard. "You have no right to hit anyone." Tiffany attempted to hit her too, but Marek stepped in between them.

"Damn bitch! You faked being innocent when you were first brought in here and look where you are now. Dalton's bitch!"

"Take her to her room, Marek! And make sure she goes back there after every client she has. She's far too unstable. I don't want her around the other girls."

Tiffany was forced out of the room while cursing and screaming.

"Be careful not to disappear, like Julia!"

The girl's words echoed in the hallway, and Chloe hurried to close the door behind them. She knew the girl was right, but she also knew she had no other choice, so she swallowed her words and turned to the girls. She had to stay calm and do what Dalton had asked her to do.

"Hi! My name is E… Chloe! I'm here to guide you in this new lifestyle."

"You mean, you'll teach us how to prostitute ourselves!" Said the girl who Tiffany had slapped a few moments ago. Her cheek was still red.

"What's your name?" Chloe asked the girl gently.

"Ellen!" The girl looked at the floor as she answered.

"Most of us were brought here in the same way as you, Ellen. I have agreed to take Julia's place because Dalton forced me to do it, not because I wanted to. And I'm also sure that Tiffany has been forced by Dalton to do certain unpleasant things too. I don't want you to think I'm defending him, but we have to understand that we are alone here and only have each other and nothing more! I can't stop all the things that Dalton will force you to do, but I promise you that I will do my best to keep you safe and help you get through this whole situation as well as possible. I took Julie's place, but I'm not her. Please believe me and try to rely on me for whatever you need."

Chloe heard the footsteps of Dalton's man and quickly changed the subject, sending the girls to use the equipment.

"Let's get some exercises done!"

The girls looked at her surprised, some distrustful, others with hope. Chloe let them sit where they wanted to, then answered their questions regarding the exercises one by one.

In the following days, the girls had the same routine. Chloe learned to run the business, which made Dalton very happy, so he continued to bring more and more girls. Some came thinking that they would have a better life. Others came beaten and covered bruises. Chloe tried not to get attached to any of them, but listened to their stories and encouraged them. Dalton always told her that she had to be tougher with them or they wouldn't listen to her. And if things didn't go well, only she would suffer.

One day, Dalton appeared with a girl stained with blood and misery. Her pale pink dress was torn in several places. Her straight blonde reached her waist. Her cheap makeup was smudged, and her mouth was swollen. The girl had been cruelly beaten and did not appear to be more than fifteen years old.

"You promised me you wouldn't!" Chloe stood up from where she was drinking her coffee and rushed to Dalton. The man let go of the child, who remained in the same place, her eyes lost, while he avoided Chloe attempts to hit him.

"You're no one worth making promises to! You are just like everyone else."

Dalton pushed her, and Chloe fell next to the girl who had fainted. She looked at her with pity and would have given anything for her not to go through what was happening.

"She's just a kid. How old is she?"

"I don't know, it doesn't matter. She is as good as you or the others. By the way her name is Kim." Dalton whistled as he spoke, and Chloe felt him begin to get angry. "Start preparing her. We'll put her up for auction with the others. I need to get rid of her as soon as possible."

"She's a minor." Chloe stood up, trying to look confident in front of the man. „You told me you wouldn't bring children here, and that's exactly what you're doing. I give up your stupid game. I give up our agreement. You can take care of them and prepare them by yourself."

Dalton slapped her hard on the face, and blood flowed from her lower lip.

"If you don't take care of her, you'll regret it! You know very well that my threats are not in vain. You choose who's going to suffer and get hurt." Dalton began to look at her with desire, and the girl swallowed hard while he said it again:

"You or her… You or her…"

She did not realize how long she had been stuck there with the man's words echoing in her head, even after he left the room.

She came out of a trance and approached the child who seemed unconscious.

"Wake up!"

The girl finally opened her eyes, and Chloe looked into the bluest eyes she had ever seen. The girl blinked a few times and whispered heavily,

"Help!" Chloe watched her fall unconscious again and shouted to Marek.

"Marek, please help me get the young lady to my room."

He took the child in his arms and went to the elevator, with Chloe following behind them. Marek always met Chloe's requirements, and although he didn't seem to be following her, he was always by her side. The only time he had spoken to her was the day he asked her to accept Dalton's proposal.

Chloe thought his boss asked him to intimidate her, but after a while, she realized that it had been the wisest advice she had ever received. She had to try to get closer to him somehow. Bloody images of Andrew came to her mind. She didn't want him to meet the same fate as Andrew, but at the same time, she had to do something to stop Dalton from selling the new girl.

They got off the elevator on Chloe's floor, and when they got to her room, she stepped aside and motioned for the man to enter. He did so and put the little girl on the bed, then waited quietly next to them.

"Fill the tub with warm water, please!" Marek went to the bathroom and did what he was asked, then went back to the room and waited until Chloe took off all the girl's clothes, then took her in her arms and headed for the bathroom. Chloe began to soap her gently, and as she removed the dirt, she wanted more and more to be able to help the child escape that hell.

Marks, scratches and pinches covered her entire body, and

she had small round burns on her back.

The child did not open her eyes, and Chloe began to worry about it. Her pulse was weak, and that moment Chloe looked at Marek helplessly. The man picked the girl up, and after Chloe wrapped her in a towel, he took her to bed.

"Wrap her up and sit next to her. I'll be right back!"

The man's pleasant voice was gentle and contrasted with his body, and Chloe did exactly as he told her to. When he came back, the girl took the child's pulse again.

"Her pulse is very weak. We need to call a doctor."

Marek nodded.

"Dalton would never allow us to call someone from outside. And the one in charge of our girls gave up some time ago."

"And yet we have to find a doctor somehow. Her pulse is weak, she may die if we are not doing anything."

Marek approached the girl and brought to her mouth the glass that he had in his hand.

"Dalton will never risk anything for her. He'd rather let her die."

The child began to move, and when she felt the fluid in her mouth, she began to cough.

"We cannot let her be sold. There must be a solution for her to get out of here without Dalton realizing it."

The child finally opened her eyes, and Marek continued to hold her glass until she drank everything. He then stood up and pulled Chloe aside as he whispered bluntly,

"You have to understand once and for all that you can't help her. Or any of them. Don't give hope to the girls anymore. Understand that this game is not about you or about them. Who do you care more about? Dalton will be ruthless this time."

The man closed the door behind him, and Chloe was left

alone with the child, who looked at her sadly.

"How are you feeling?" The child crouched down when Chloe sat down by her side. She closed her eyes and squeezed her mouth in a thin, fine line. Chloe kept talking to her, "What's your name? Talk to me, little one, please! How old are you?"

Chloe continued to ask the girl questions but received no answers. The girl's haunted gaze made a shiver run down her spine.

"Drink this!" She handed the girl a glass of water and the pill Marek had brought to her. She continued to sit next to her until she began to breathe regularly, signifying that she was asleep. Then, Chloe left the room in search of Dalton. He was in his office with Marek, who was reporting to him.

"I want to talk to you!" Chloe headed to the bar from which she got a glass and poured herself some brandy. She drank it in one gulp, under the eyes of the two men.

"You heard Chloe's wish. Leave us alone, Marek!"

"Yes, Sir!"

Marek left the room without looking at her, and Chloe poured herself another glass, then sat down on the free chair at Dalton's desk.

"Who is she? Why did you kidnap her?"

Dalton looked at her mockingly.

"These details are none of your business, my dear! Your job is to take care of the girls, not to ask questions about them."

"I don't want to do it anymore, not as long as you bring children here."

"This business will bring us a lot of money, no matter how old the girls brought here are. They come to produce. Soon we will have a few more, all minors, and you will make sure that they fit in and learn everything you have learned from Julia."

"You're wrong. I won't do it. I'd rather die than do it."

Dalton got up and approached Chloe, who began to tremble with fear. The man's attitude scared her. He didn't seem angry, but the girl knew that there was a hot volcano under the apparent calmness.

"If you think that death is the cruelest way to end things, you are sorely mistaken, my dear! Did you take care of the girl? Did you take that shit off of her?"

Chloe caught his eye and turned white. She grabbed him by the sleeve and begged him:

"Don't touch her, Dalton, please! Don't do this. The girl is still in shock."

Dalton smiled naughtily at her and answered hoarsely.

"The girl is not a virgin anymore, and as she is mine, I can do whatever I want with her. What room is she in?"

"Take me in her place." Chloe said the words with difficulty.

She was shocked by the thoughts that went through her mind, but she knew she could not let Dalton be with the new girl.

"I'll ask Marek where she is. It looks like you don't want to cooperate." He was ready to open the door, and Chloe rushed to him. She began to punch him in the back as she shouted softly:

"Don't you hear? Leave her alone. I'm here. You are a coward. You always want to take advantage of defenseless people. Coward!"

Dalton turned, and Chloe noticed the change in his gaze, and when his fist hit her in the stomach, she thought she would faint from all that pain. And although she knew what was coming, she was at the same time relieved that Dalton would not head to her room.

"I'll give you exactly what you're looking for, Sunshine!" The man began to take off his belt and, after doing so, picked up

Chloe and slammed her on his desk and as he hit her, he spoke harshly to her

"You forget who the boss is here. You think you can come and threaten me whenever you feel like it? You're a bitch like all the others. Don't forget your place when you are in front of me."

Dalton continued to hit her, causing her pain. When the girl felt like she would faint, she felt hands tearing her thin dress and the man making room between her legs."

"No!" The girl began to scream when the man bit her breasts and tried to push him off of her.

"I told you that one day you'd come to me by yourself. I hope you are ready to bear the consequences of your recklessness."

Dalton continued to touch and bite her. Chloe gasped in pain, and with each scream, she caused more pleasure for the man. "I liked you from the first moment I saw you. Night after night, I imagined how it would be to possess you and make you mine in every possible way."

"I hate you!" Chloe looked him in the eye as she whispered the words.

The man began to laugh and put his hand between her legs:

"And yet you are here, at my mercy!"

The man's hands moved up and down between the girl's legs as he kissed her neck. The sooner you learn how things are between us, the better off you will be. You are not able to set conditions or ask too much. Because, my dear, things will always be done the way I want, with or without your will."

"You're a bastard! One day you will pay for everything you're doing!"

Dalton seemed more and more amused. He turned her abruptly, and after making room between her legs, penetrated her.

Chloe gritted her teeth and remained in that position without whining or hesitating, so as not to provoke Dalton too much. With each touch of the man, she felt more exhausted and, at the same time, more disappointed by her cowardice.

When he finished and closed his pants, Chloe leaned over, lifted her panties, and tightened her torn dress. Dalton raised his hand to her face, and Chloe looked him in the eye with hatred.

"Be careful how you behave in the next few days. More girls will come. The auction is closer than you think, and I want everything to be ready."

Chloe hurried to her room. In the empty elevator, she started crying. Physical pain was unimportant at that time. She had managed to stop Dalton from touching the girl in her room. But she did not know how long she would be able to do it. She did not want to accept the idea that the girl could go through what she had. To be auctioned and sold to who knows who. Men would not care that she was just a child. They would take from her what they wanted. Then they would get rid of her.

Lost in her thoughts, she opened the door of her room and looked at the still sleeping girl. She went into the shower and stayed under the water until her body couldn't stand the hot water anymore and she felt that she no longer had the strength to stand up. She put a robe on and sat down in the chair next to the bed where the little girl was still sleeping.

"Chloe, wake up! Marek was shaking her lightly, and the girl opened her eyes."

There was no one in the bed next to her.

"Where is she?" Chloe got up and headed for the bathroom, where there was no one. She angrily turned to Marek. "What did you do to her? Tell me, where is she, damn it?"

"Calm down!" The man grabbed her hands because she

would not stop hitting him and pushed her to the bed where she fell. "A doctor came to see her, and then she was brought to the empty room next to yours."

Marek spoke softly to her, and when the girl walked to the door, he stepped in between her and the door, then handed her a round, colorless box with small colored pills in it. Dalton says to give her two a day.

"Ecstasy! These will not help her forget what she went through over the last days. Chloe threw the pillbox on the bed."

"I also brought you coffee."

Marek showed the cup of coffee that was on the bedside. "You know, Miss, my dad didn't mind repeating a saying to me every time we drank coffee together and he saw me knocked down by worries: 'There are two types of people in this world: the smart ones who don't put sugar in coffee and the others.'"

Marek turned around and left while Chloe was sitting down on the chair.

Chapter Seven

"Julia would never have sacrificed herself for us!"

"I heard the new girl is only fifteen. Dalton is such a bastard."

Chloe grabbed the doorknob and opened the gym door, interrupting the discussion between the girls, who remained silent and hurried to the machines.

"Hi!"

Chloe stopped in front of them and measured them one by one. They looked tired. Some of them had deep dark circles and red eyes, probably due to lack of sleep or the drugs they consumed.

"You heard right! Dalton has begun to bring in minors, fifteen-year-olds, like Kim. And if the business goes the way he wants, he won't stop bringing in minors. Kim was unconscious, she had been raped, and cruelly beaten when she arrived here. The last time I saw her, she was still in shock. This morning she was taken to another room, and Dalton asked me to give her ecstasy twice a day. Last night he wanted to go to her, but I managed to stop him, and I hope he'll never get to her room because we know how violent he can be. And I don't know how long she will resist this way."

The girls looked at her with distrust and began to whisper to each other,

"It's not possible!"

"Dalton is a bastard!"

"He forces us to prostitute ourselves for him, and now he wants to force children to do so as well."

"We need to do something…"

The girls all talked at the same time, and Chloe had to interrupt them:

"I need time to find a way to help the new girl to get out of here. The auction will be soon, and Dalton will try to get to her first. I saw the way she looked at him when he brought her in. And last night, he made it clear to me that nothing could stop him from doing what he has in mind with her. I need you to stop him from doing it…"

The girls fell silent and looked at her, scared. All of them knew what it meant to be visited by Dalton, and it was clear that no one enjoyed it.

"How do you want us to help her escape? You think we haven't tried to escape from this hell?"

"I'll try to contact someone outside. I don't trust the police, but I know I have to do something for Kim."

"And if you fail and Dalton finds out?" Tiffany stood up and approached Chloe. "If he finds out, he won't hesitate to kill you, and then he'll take revenge on us."

"I'll take it all on myself if…"

Tiffany started laughing hysterically.

"You think you know Dalton? Just because he fucked you twice. You hardened him a little, and when you saw how violent he was, you got scared. Look at my ear!"

The girl pulled her hair back and turned her right ear to Chloe. The top of it was cut.

"He did this to me!" Charlenne lifted her blouse, and the girls were able to see small cuts on the girl's abdomen. "And he put cigarettes out on her hands one night when he came here drunk," said Charlenne pointing at the short blonde girl. "And we're not the only ones. Over time Dalton has abused a bunch of girls."

"The man is a sadist. He likes to hurt women. He gets aroused by the pain of others."

Chloe was trembling when she saw the hatred in the girls' eyes. Dalton had hurt them too much. She put her hand on Tiffany's shoulder and said,

"I'm sorry, Tiffany! I'm sorry for what you endured because of him. But if we don't stop Dalton, we'll end up dead like Julia."

"We'll die if we help you, or maybe even worse..."

The girls looked scared, and although Chloe understood why, she needed their help.

"What can be worse in this case? Dalton will continue to harm you. He will not stop bringing in children or killing innocent women. But, if we can get in touch with someone we can trust, maybe we'll be able to expose Dalton."

The girls made a circle and began to whisper to each other, then at one point, Tiffany looked at Chloe and said:

"We need time to decide."

"Okay! The lesson is over. I'll be waiting for you tomorrow at the same time." Chloe approached the door, and before opening it, she said, "If you don't want to get involved, keep your mouth shut, or I'll make sure to make Dalton believe you're plotting against me. I have no other solution. I don't agree with what he's doing, and I'll do anything to stop him."

There was silence in the room, and Chloe left. She closed the door behind her and headed for the elevator, where Marek was coming out. The girl looked at him sadly, and when she reached him, she whispered:

"In the morning, when you told me those things, you really wanted to warn me, no?"

Marek looked down at the ground and spoke harshly to her:

"The new girl woke up and started screaming. Dalton was heading for her. I thought maybe you were interested!"

Chloe got angry and shouted at him:

"Where is Dalton right now?"

"Calm down. You're not helping Kim or yourself now. Dalton doesn't have to see you like that. He sent me for you!"

"Take me to them, please!"

The girl looked at him kindly, and Marek nodded, then turned to the elevator. When they reached the girl's room, Chloe rushed to the door and opened it.

Dalton was sitting by the girl's bed, pulling the blanket she was wrapped in.

"Leave her alone!"

Dalton stopped and turned to Chloe, looking angrily at her. "What?"

Dalton slapped the girl in the face, then pushed her next to Kim, who was crying. "I warned you that if you didn't take care of her, I'll do it myself. Time is running out. The auction is approaching, and I don't see any change."

Chloe stood up and tried to take control of the situation while talking calmly,

"I'll take care of her. I promise! I told you last night I would. The child's just woken up now. It's not her fault. She's just scared."

"Very well, take care of this, and we'll talk about your tasks soon." The man's tone made Chloe shudder, and she breathed a sigh of relief when she saw Dalton walking away with Marek.

"He left!" Chloe pulled the blanket, and the girl stopped

crying and pulled her head out of the blanket.

"Who is he?" The child's voice was frail.

Chloe sat down on the bed next to her and began to talk softly to her:

"His name is Dalton, he…"

Chloe paused and looked at the girl, who looked back at her with big eyes. Her face was all bruised. Chloe's heart ached as thinking about all that child had gone through. "Dalton is the one who forces us into prostitution."

"Who are you?"

"My real name is Emily Growdy. I worked as a secretary for Dalton, but when I discovered that he was dealing in human trafficking, I tried to resign. I was abducted instead and brought here. Dalton was always one step ahead of me. He knew everything about me. He knew I had no one to look for me, and he knew when I discovered the truth."

"What happened next?" The child interrupted Chloe's thoughts, she was overwhelmed by her memories.

"Dalton sold me at an auction to a Grecian. He bought me to have sex with his brother, but he made me his in the end. I stayed at one of his houses for a few months. Everything was fine, or so I thought, until one day Dalton showed up with the wife of the man who had bought me. They took me from there against my will, and I came back here, where Dalton forced me to take Julia's place, the woman who was training the girls before me."

"What happened to her? Is she still here?"

The child listened carefully to all the details.

"She was killed! By Dalton!"

"And your Greek man?"

Chloe was surprised by the girl's question. Since she came back to that hell, she hadn't had time to think about Alexander.

All she knew was that the man had a pregnant wife at home, a woman who cared about him and was able to keep him by her side.

"I don't know anything about him!"

She thought she would probably never hear from him again. The man had not cared much about her. He had drugged her. The feelings she thought she had for him disappeared when she found out that Alexander was drugging her with that tea. The man was no different from Dalton. They both deserved to go to hell for what they had done to her.

"What will happen to me?"

Chloe approached the girl and grabbed her hand.

"Dalton is forcing me to prepare you for the auction."

The child looked her bravely in the eye and asked,

"Will you?"

Chloe nodded and smiled sadly at her.

"The bruises on your body, he did this to you? It doesn't matter!" Chloe wiped the tears from the girl's face. "I have to get you out of here. I'll find a way to do this!"

She stood up and started walking around the room.

"You'd better not!"

Chloe stopped abruptly and approached Kim,

"What do you want to say?"

"I don't want you to save me! I can't be saved! She began to cry and put her head back on the blanket."

"Don't you want to tell me how you got into this situation? What happened to you, little girl? Talk to me, Kim! Please!"

Chloe pulled on the girl's blanket.

"I can't imagine what you went through, nor can I compare what happened to you with what happened to me. But I can assure you, however, that I will do my best to protect you and try to get you out of here."

"There's nothing you can do for me!" she said.

Kim sighed, and her voice faded when she began to talk, "My father sold me to Dalton after raping me for years."

Chloe was shocked to hear what the girl was saying. She did not understand how her father could have harmed her so much. How could he be so cruel to her?

"I…" Chloe couldn't find her words. She couldn't imagine what Kim had suffered.

"I want you to promise me something." The child opened her eyes and looked Chloe in the eye as she grabbed her hands. "When the time comes, you will let me go. You won't do anything for me. I don't want you to risk yourself for me, please!"

The girl's request left Chloe speechless. The girl did not want to escape, and she had asked her to do nothing about the situation she was in. She was probably referring to the auction where she was to be sold. She was wrong if she thought she would be better off with the man who would buy her. She didn't understand why the child was asking her that.

"I can't do that, Kim! I have to do something for you. Otherwise, I will never forgive myself."

The child began to cry louder and shouted frightenedly:

"You do not understand! I can't go back to him. I'd rather die…"

Chloe hugged her until Kim calmed and began to breathe normally.

"Everything will be fine, I promise. You'll never go back to that monster. It'll be fine, my little one. It'll be fine…"

Chloe held her in her arms until the girl fell asleep.

That night she slept next to Kim. When Marek told her Dalton was gone, Chloe asked him to take care of the girls and remained with Kim. The next day she made sure the girl ate something, and when she fell asleep, Chloe left the room. At the door there was Marek.

"Let me know if she wakes up, please!"

"Yes, Miss!"

"Call me Chloe, please! And let me know when Dalton returns."

Chloe headed to the gym, where the girls were waiting for her. When she came in, Tiffany tried to say something, but Chloe spoke first,

"I don't know how long I'll be able to keep Dalton away from Kim. Those who want to help me, stay here. Those who don't are free to leave.

The girls did not move and Chloe, with all the courage she had, began to talk to them:

"The girl was raped for years by her father. She was later sold to Dalton. She was so lost that last night she made me promise her that I would not risk anything to help her get out of here. She wants to be sold and doesn't want to go back to her father. We don't only have to help her get out of here. We have to find her a place to live, a safe place where Dalton can't find her."

Charlenne approached her and handed her a pink note.

"Here's a friend's phone number. After I was brought here, it was the only number I could remember. I never had a chance to contact him. He deals with such cases, and I'm sure he'll help you. You have to memorize the phone number and then throw the paper away because if Dalton finds it, he'll kill us both."

Chloe did so, and after memorizing the phone number, Chloe read the name. Mike Statham. It sounded familiar, but she didn't know from were.

Tiffany started talking, and the girls started listened to her

168

carefully,

"Tomorrow night is poker night. Dalton usually plays until he loses money, then gets drunk and comes to my room, where he stays until morning. He says that it cheers him up to hurt me when he loses money. My plan is to pick up his phone after he falls asleep. You have to take care of the rest."

"Does he usually drink something when he comes to you?"

When Tiffany said that he did, Chloe continued,

"We can put an ecstasy pill in his drink. He may not fall asleep, but it will certainly make him feel euphoric. I'm sure he won't be as violent."

"What are we going to do about Marek? He always guards Dalton when he sleeps in my room. Thrisa's voice was heard, and the girls began to speak all at the same time.

"We should put a pill in his drink too."

"Or keep him busy, one of us has to call him to our room."

Charlenne raised her hand and said:

"Marek will come to my room. I'll make sure I keep him busy all night. When the girls looked at her with distrust, the girl continued, "He likes me. We talk sometimes. The first time he came, he wanted to pay me, but I refused."

"Very well, Charlenne keeps Marek in her room, and you make sure you get Dalton's phone."

"The other girls will sit quietly in their rooms, attentive to any noise. If something happens, I want you to stay in your rooms. And if Dalton finds out about our plan, I want you to blame me. You can say that I forced you or that you did not know what it was about. I don't want anything to happen to you."

The girls nodded, and Chloe motioned for them to return to what they were doing.

"Someone's coming! If anything changes, let me know, and

watch out for the cameras. There are very few places where they are not placed. God help us!"

The door opened, and Marek entered the room.

"Chloe, Dalton is waiting for you all in the living room in an hour. He wants you to bring Kim too."

Chloe looked at the girls, scared, and said harshly,

"You heard; the lesson is over. In an hour we will see each other in the dining room where you will meet the new girl. I hope you treat her well, or you will have to deal with me."

Chloe wanted to look harshly at the girls, but inside her a voice was shouting for help. She then headed for the door and waited for the girls to come out, then followed them. She set out for the room where Kim was sleeping, disgusted by the thought that she had to prepare her for Dalton. She hated Dalton so much for what he was forcing her to do, and she was hoping that the plan would succeed with all her heart.

The evening went well. After Chloe told the girls that they would all meet in the dining room, she had to find a dress that would cover her as much as possible and at the same time make sure Dalton would like it too.

When they arrived at the dining room, she sat down next to Kim and tried to turn Dalton's attention to her all evening. The new girl answered syllabically every time the other girls tried to talk to her and she looked at them all with pity.

In her long black dress and with her hair of the same color, she looked much more mature than she was. The blue eyes had something special in them. She was so beautiful and so innocent, she didn't deserve her fate.

Dalton sat at the head of the table and, like every afternoon, asked the girls questions about the business. How it went and if they needed anything. When they finished, Dalton set the girls free to retire, except for Chloe and little Kim.

"Stand up and turn around!" Dalton told the child, who seemed stuck in her chair.

"Kim!" Chloe whispered her name, and when the girl looked up, she continued, "Do what Dalton says!"

The child got up and did so. She was tall and thin, exactly the kind of girl Dalton was looking for.

"Have you thought of a more exotic name for her?" Dalton asked Chloe, and when she nodded, he continued to speak, "I guess we can call her Kim. It will be easier for her. She told you that her father had sold her to me for a few bottles of whiskey? She is lucky I came across him by mistake. The old man wanted a drink, and he was waiting at the corner of a street, looking for customers for her. Of course, after he enjoyed her first." Dalton began to laugh loudly and Kim began to tremble.

"It's time for her to take her pill. I'll leave her in her room, then go take a bath. If you want to come you are welcome."

Chloe turned to the child, who kept shaking, and took her hand.

Dalton raised his eyebrows and measured Chloe from head to toe lustfully.

"Looks like you're starting to realize your place. Go to your room. Maybe I'll follow you soon."

Chloe hurried out, and as she did, she heard the sound of a drink pouring into a glass. Dalton had been drinking throughout dinner, and the girl hoped that if he had got drunk, he would retire to his room to sleep. On the other hand, she knew that he would make her suffer if he came to her room drunk. So, when he invited her, she had no choice. She saw the spark that ignited in his eyes as the child began to tremble. She acted quickly to keep him from thinking about Kim.

Chloe was scared when she heard a bang. She thought she was dreaming, and as she got out of bed, she tried to calm down. When she heard the second shot, she ran to Kim's room. The images of Andrew being shot came to her mind, but she quickly let them go as she entered the child's room. Kim hiding in her blanket and shaking.

"Kim!" Chloe shouted at her, and the girl pulled her head out of the blanket, looking at her scared." Go to my room and hide in the bathroom. Don't come out of there until I come for you. I'll try to get back as soon as I can."

"Don't go! Stay with me. Kim whispered the words as they both left the room."

"I have to do it. I don't know what's going on. I have to go find out." Chloe pushed the girl to her room and then headed for the elevator. Before entering, she shouted to the child warning her, "Stay calm in the room until I return."

"Don't go there."

The girl looked at her scared, and Chloe pressed one of the elevator buttons. As the doors closed, she saw Kim coming towards her and shouting for her to come back. She knew she had to do it, but she couldn't stay calm while Dalton was possibly hurting someone. Halfway through the elevator, she met Marek, who was also searching for her.

"What happened?"

"Dalton went crazy, shot Tiffany, and ordered me to take you to her room."

Marek looked at her angrily from a height of almost two meters. The man was upset and could have crushed her without putting in too much effort. His tone and the news of Tiffany's death made Chloe freeze. Marek abruptly pushed her towards the dead girl's room.

"Hurry up. Dalton called all the girls to Tiffany's room and didn't seem too patient."

When they got close, Chloe heard the girls' sighs, and when she entered the room, she was shocked by the cruelty with which the girl had been killed. Tiffany was tied to the four pillars of the bed and had a disfigured face. She had a hole in her and the whole bed was soaked in blood.

"It's all your fault."

Dalton's voice made her look back at him while trembling hard. The man was sitting in a chair with a glass in one hand and a gun in the other. He was dressed in the same clothes he had worn for dinner that night.

"I gave you the chance to do the right thing, and you transformed everything into a mess. You tried to betray me twice, and every time someone died because of you. So, give me a reason not to kill you. Even if I know that the only one who has to die is you. You are the traitor!"

"Do it!"

Chloe looked up, defying him. Dalton approached her and slapped her hard. Chloe fell to the ground. She had blood in her mouth. She spat at the feet of the man who had hit her in the face.

Dalton hit the girl every time she tried to stand up as she put herself in front of little Kim, who didn't heed her advice to hide, and followed her to Tiffany's room.

"The first time you managed to get Andrew to help you, he helped you at the price of his life. Now you managed to convince them to do all the crap you've been planning, and because of you, I lost a precious bitch, one that brought me quite a lot of money."

Dalton hit the girl every time she tried to stand up as she put herself in front of little Kim. Finally, he stopped hurting Chloe and motioned for the girl standing in the doorway to approach.

When the child came to closer, she looked at Chloe and whispered resignedly to her:

"Chloe, I told you not to go!" She then continued to walk until she reached Dalton.

"You shouldn't have tried to save little Kim. Right, little girl? You don't want to be saved. When your father brought you to my car, you begged me to take you with me. You see, Chloe, the girl has been raped by her father and his friends for a long time. And when the girl found a way to make it stop, she did not hesitate. The night the old man wanted to sell her to me, he was dead drunk. And after he told me everything he did to the girl, he also had the guts to ask me for money. Do you know what I gave him in return? I bet you couldn't guess even if we stayed here all night. I tied him to a tree and handed his daughter a gun. She emptied it into the old man while he was screaming, begging for forgiveness, in less than a few moments."

Dalton began to laugh and then pulled Kim close to him and kissed her. Chloe, who finally managed to stand up, turned her head to the frightened girls. They were all beautiful and different in their own ways, but they all had one thing in common: Dalton. That monster had taken their lives, and he was doing what he wanted with them. They all knew his anger. They were all marked in some way by him.

Her gaze fell on the bed and Tiffany's dead body. Because of her, two people had died. Because of her, the child, who had shot a father who had abused her for years, would be punished along with the other girls. And it was all her fault, just because she didn't dare to act against the monster earlier.

"You think I did it for her?" Chloe began to laugh hysterically, and Dalton pulled away from the trembling girl. "I did it for myself. I couldn't stand your touches anymore. I hate you, and I hated you from the very first moment we met."

The man was beginning to lose control once more and Chloe kept laughing and talking:

"Look at you. Julia told me something about you before she put me up for auction. Your father enjoyed making your mother suffer. From him, you learned to be a sadist. And your mother had drowned her bitterness in alcohol and fucked whoever she could find. So, you probably grew up with the impression that all women are like your mother and that you, as a man, have to punish them. Just like your father was doing…"

Chloe saw Dalton's hand pointing the gun at her, and she closed her eyes, resigned.

She heard two simultaneous shots. When she opened her eyes, Kim collapsed on her. Chloe grabbed her in her arms and began to cry.

"Kim, why did you do that, little girl? I didn't want to be saved either. I can't live with all this guilt on my shoulders. Kim, don't fall asleep, little one, please! An ambulance, call an ambulance!"

The girls had gathered all around them, and when Chloe looked up, she saw Dalton falling too. She then looked at Marek talking on the phone and Dalton shouting at him with his last breaths that he would kill him when he recovered, and then she understood everything.

Dalton was the first to shoot, and while Kim threw herself in front of her, Marek shot Dalton. The girl got up and stood in front of Dalton, who kept screaming at Marek and asking for help at the same time. She took the gun from Dalton's powerless hands and with her eyes closed, she pulled the trigger. When she felt Marek's hands on her, the girl opened her eyes and let go of the gun. She saw Dalton, who was dead, and then Kim smiling with

175

her pale face.

"He won't hurt anyone anymore." Chloe went to Kim. The girls were all looking at her with fear and admiration.

"Forgive me!" Kim managed to give her a last hug.

"You have to forgive me. I promised to protect you, and I failed."

The two girls cried, and when Marek approached her, Kim quickly whispered to her:

"You have to let me go! It's time for me to leave…"

"I can't do it! Please, Kim, don't do this to me!"

Chloe cried and cried over the girl's body.

"We have to go. The police will be here in a few minutes. There are cameras everywhere. They'll see you killed Dalton. You have to hide!"

Chloe looked at the man who had saved her.

"Thank you! I'll stay by her side."

"No!" Kim took her hand, and Chloe looked at her. "Go with him! Thank you for everything you've done for me, but you have to let me go. Go Chloe, and never forget that I know you just wanted to save me."

Chloe watched the child urge her to leave as her life flowed from her body, and then she understood what the girl had asked her to promise her in the room the day they talked about what had happened to her. Kissing Kim lightly on the forehead, then getting up and looking at the girls urging her to leave, she whispered to them,

"Thank you!" Then she went out after Marek without looking back.

The moment she stepped into the garage full of cars, she felt empty. She got into Marek's car, and when he started the engine, she closed her eyes.

"The people that Dalton was working for will look for us, and the police are on our trail." The man's voice made Chloe open her eyes.

"I guess we have to hide for a while. Do you have any idea where we can go?"

"I have a friend who has a country house in Bruges. What do you say?"

"I always wanted to go there."

The two fell silent, and Chloe realized one thing at that moment that Emily Growdy wasn't alive anymore. She had died when she was kidnapped by Dalton, and she had to remain dead.

As for her little brother, she would send money to Mother Davies to take care of him as she had promised. She could not risk his life, and if she did go to see him, she knew bad things could happen.

So, she was going to disappear for a while until things eventually calmed down. Then she'd come back and make sure everyone involved in Dalton's business would pay. She also wanted to find the girls and make sure each and every one of them was safe. Now she could only hope that the police would let them return to their homes. The police, the law enforcement. Chloe clenched her fists and angrily promised herself that she would never trust them again.

The car left the town and entered a country road, and Chloe opened the window for some fresh air. Free, she was free to do whatever she wanted to do. She was free to seek justice for Andrew, Tiffany, and little Kim. Tears of relief began to flow down her cheeks. Tired and full of pain, she closed her eyes again and fell asleep, with the man to her left watching her with admiration.